The Duchess Games

The Dainty Devils
Book 1

By Alyxandra Harvey

Dragonblade Publishing, Inc. is an imprint of Kathryn Le Veque Novels, Inc.
P.O. Box 23
Moreno Valley, CA 92556
ceo@dragonbladepublishing.com

Produced in the United States of America

First Edition June 2023
Trade Paperback Edition

ARE YOU SIGNED UP FOR DRAGONBLADE'S BLOG?

You'll get the latest news and information on exclusive giveaways, exclusive excerpts, coming releases, sales, free books, cover reveals and more.

Check out our complete list of authors, too!

No spam, no junk. That's a promise!

Sign Up Here

www.dragonbladepublishing.com

Dearest Reader;

Thank you for your support of a small press. At Dragonblade Publishing, we strive to bring you the highest quality Historical Romance from some of the best authors in the business. Without your support, there is no 'us', so we sincerely hope you adore these stories and find some new favorite authors along the way.

Happy Reading!

CEO, Dragonblade Publishing

Additional Dragonblade books by Author Alyxandra Harvey

The Dainty Devils Series
The Duchess Games (Book 1)

The Cinderella Society Series
How to Marry an Earl (Book 1)
How to Marry a Duke (Book 2)
How to Marry a Viscount (Book 3)

Chapter One

CAITRIONA SPARROW WAS certain that ladies did not sweat. They perspired. Or *glowed*. Or something equally absurd.

Cat was *sweating*.

August should not be so *hot*.

More to the point, it was cruel to pack this many people into a room, while forcing them to wear layers of petticoats and gloves and starched cravats. Cat's sister Viola floated through the crowd, fresh as a lily, her muslin gown billowing like mist at her feet. Cat had made do with altering one of their mother's old gowns. It was a lovely blue. It was also better suited to crisp autumn days at the beach.

She would cut off her own arm for a crisp autumn day at the beach.

But alas, it was bonbons and cheese carved into roses in a room papered with silk and steeped in perfume. The windows were shut because the dowager duchess objected to the saltiness of the wind. It was not dignified. Too *Cornish*.

Cat failed to see how melting into a puddle on the very fine carpet was dignified.

But then she had never been particularly fashionable. Dignity was for people who did not spend a great deal of their time crawling through haylofts after abandoned kittens or coaxing stray dogs out of mud puddles. She and her sister Viola had faced broken bones, several feral cats, and once, a regrettably dead body washed up on the beach.

Not to mention her other, somewhat less legal, hobbies.

But they had never, it had to be said, faced a house party on the very grand estate of an English Lord. Not just a lord, in fact, but a *duke*.

The Duke of Tremaine, to be precise.

Why did it have to be *Callum*?

Cat forced herself to focus on the bead of sweat currently running down her spine. Even the poor vicar, handsome and muscular as he was, looked as though he might faint from the heat. His cravat had wilted, but if he took off his thick coat, there might be a stampede. He was single and good looking and there was only one duke, after all. And a vast number of ladies.

Cat had never seen half so many aristocrats in all her life. Small wonder as she had spent the entirety of that life in the fishing village of Little Crumpet. She lifted her glass to him in a toast of solidarity. He blinked back at her. Spinsters lurking by the garden doors did not generally toast men. Or fan themselves quite so vigorously.

Where was Callum, anyway? They were cooking together in this cake-colored room for his benefit. He should be sweating with them. Although if she were to catch his eye, she might have to worry about the state of her hair, and if her forehead was glistening (it absolutely was).

Caitriona Sparrow catching the eye of a duke. Even this duke.

Especially this duke.

It was laughable. She had not seen him in years. In fact, until they stepped into this parlor mere moments ago, she hadn't even known he was back in Cornwall. He was hardly going to pay her a social call.

He had once.

A long time ago.

There was easily two dozen people mingling under the painted ceiling. Marble angels flew around the fireplace which was filled with flowers in deference to the heat. There was an alarming number of lions on every surface: crystal figurines, paintings, gold candlesticks. Someone had clearly told the dowager that lions were stately.

Lady Summer, the duke's sister, greeted everyone with a smile and a promise that ices would be brought out shortly. She was beautiful and cheerful—everything the Tremaine title disdained. Cat remembered that much. The ladies murmured appreciatively. The vicar nearly wept.

Viola made her way back to Cat. "Are you very miserable?" she asked, sympathetically.

Cat forced a smile. "Of course not."

"Liar. Your cheeks are red."

Some women went temptingly pink with heat, glistened like iced teacakes. Cat did not.

"It's this dress," she admitted with a wry smile. Never mind the hundreds of chores she should be attending to instead of standing here sweltering. Or the thousand details that needed to be worked out if she was going to become Little Crumpet's next criminal mastermind. The last criminal mastermind had stolen raisin buns. He had been all of six years old.

Viola's answering smile was amused but also tinged with a familiar kind of sadness. "Mother loved that dress. But then, she was always cold."

They had enough money to fake a wardrobe for a house party for exactly one person and it would be wasted on Caitriona. Never mind that she was long on the shelf, but she also spent most of her time with dogs and barn cats and cranky goats. Sometimes a ferret or two.

"You do look a bit queasy," Viola said. "Put your head out of the window."

"Like the family dog trying to bite the wind?" They had four dogs at last count, all of whom would have done exactly that.

Viola laughed. "You'll make me look good, at least." At twenty-three years old, with a bright smile and adorable freckles, she did not need assistance in looking her best. Even when she was not dressed like a flower.

Still, this was rather outside their purview.

Cat knew she ought not look a gift horse in the mouth. She needed access to the estate and to Callum, Duke of Tremaine. This would be much easier if he was not Callum, but instead only "His Grace." If that summer did not lie between them.

But Viola needed to make connections. Cat might love her little life in Little Crumpet, dangers notwithstanding, but Viola wanted more than the fishing village. She always had. And opportunities such as this one were scarce on the ground.

No matter what they cost her.

But a country *house party*.

Full of debutantes and lords and shoes that pinched. In her own parlor, she could fling her slippers clear across the room and curl up in a soft chair, covered in dog hair. If she did that here, the butler would toss her out on her ear.

She could do this.

She *had* to do this.

She would never have an opportunity like it again.

Even though she'd known Callum years ago, she'd only glimpsed the house from afar as a child when they dared each other to get close. The dowager duchess had instructed the footmen to run them off with hunting hounds. And possibly pelt them with stones. That might have been a story they told themselves to see who would fall back first in fear, but honestly, it seemed plausible. In fact, she might have been the one to start that rumor. She had absolutely been the one to steal the slowest dog with the limp. He did not look properly fed.

Penhallow had seemed massive back then, but if anything, it was bigger now. It prevailed over the horizon, wings opening onto other wings, into a maze of a building in the gray stone famous to Cornwall. It had stood in the same spot for over two hundred years, as evidenced in the Tudor timber framed gatehouse, the parapets, and the addition of the modern Corinthian columns. It was a lot to take in. Imposing, beautiful. Formal.

Her room in the guest wing boasted gold tassels bigger than a Christmas goose.

Her bed felt like a cloud. An actual cloud. There were even angels watching her from the ceiling, carved in relief.

It was disconcerting, to be honest.

She'd rather sleep in a fishing boat.

After the footmen finished circulating with teacups filled with ice in a variety of flavors from lemon to mint to parmesan, the dowager duchess rang a tiny silver bell. Silence fell, broken only by the clink of silver spoons on porcelain.

"I want to welcome you all to Penhallow on behalf of the duke," she said, glittering with diamonds and pearls. Cat had seen quail eggs smaller than the pearls she wore at her ears. She could buy a barrel of the best salt with a single one. Five barrels. If there was ever a proper pilchard harvest to salt, that was. There were too many people in danger of starving just a thousand meters south of where she stood, and too many sugar biscuits in this room.

"It is no secret that His Grace must marry. Nor is it a secret that I have selected only the finest families for this little party, though only those joining us from London may have seen the papers." She lifted the ironed newspaper, of which she was clearly proud.

"The finest families and us," Cat whispered to Viola, amused. They were here after having won a village lottery for an invitation to the fine house. Cat had not entered their names. She knew exactly how they had got here. And Viola didn't. Would never.

Bad enough she knew about the smuggling.

This was so much worse.

And she absolutely would not think about Callum getting married.

It was none of her business.

"We will get to know each other. A duchess must be proficient in all of the social graces, after all."

The ladies exchanged glances fraught with what might be generously called adrenaline. Less generously: battle frenzy. Cat was more accustomed to seeing it on the beach under a full moon while looking out for revenue men.

"The lady who excels at each task will sit next to His Grace at supper that night. And the lady I find *most* pleasing will open the ball on his arm."

A rustle went through the crowd. Lady Tremaine may as well have handed out swords and sabers to go with the pearls and the cravats. Parents calculated debts owed, possible dowries. Unmarried ladies went sharp with interest or disgust—and some panic—quickly hidden behind polite smiles. All in a single moment.

"Do you suppose she really means him to marry the winner?" Viola asked, her competitive streak rising to the surface. She might not have given a fig about being a duchess before now, but it had also never been an option. "I'm tired of the smell of fish."

Viola, with her kind smile and her freckles, went to extraordinary lengths to win a game, regardless of if she even wanted the prize. She was the reason they stopped playing parlor games as a family. And why their chess set, which their younger brother Matthew had carved from driftwood, was missing a queen. Viola had hurled it into the fire in a fit of pique, quickly followed by a fit of self-aware giggles. She made a new queen from the end of a rutabaga. One of the dogs proceeded to eat it.

Lady Tremaine had not come right out and said she was choosing her son's bride, but it was a fair assumption.

And if nothing else, the winner would have her blessing and his attention. And the honor of opening the ball with the first dance where if they did not catch the duke's eye—they might catch someone else's eye.

But what he thought about this whole situation was anyone's

guess. The man was unreadable, beyond appearing generally annoyed with the world at large. A stern and unyielding enigma. And that was when he was in the room. God only knew where he was right now. If he had a brain in his head, he'd be already on his way to Ireland.

The thought of Viola marrying Callum made her even queasier. She inched closer to the French doors. Could this day get any worse?

Of course, it could.

It could always get worse.

Enter Callum Winter, the eleventh Duke of Tremaine.

Unfairly, the man had grown more handsome. He was wider in the shoulders than she remembered. His dark hair swept back perfectly, as if it wouldn't dare disobey. He wore a black coat and a dark gray waistcoat, his features strong and serious. He had the air of a man who always seemed to be thinking, working problems over in his head, collecting knowledge. Utterly in control.

He surveyed the glittering crowd that stood arrested at his arrival. There was a rolled newspaper in his hand, much like the one his mother had brandished triumphantly.

"Hell no."

It was all he said before stalking right back out the door.

There was a moment of shocked silence. The duke was proper to the point of coldness, according to the whispers swirling around Cat. This was most unseemly. Unexpected. Intriguing.

As if *his* behavior was the problem here.

His mother looked as though her very expensive, very formal wig might catch fire at any moment.

"But these are no ordinary games," Lady Summer added, rising from her seat to smooth over the gossip stirring like waves under the moon. Her brown curls were caught back with sapphire pins. Lady Tremaine frowned majestically at her daughter. Were Cat Lady Summer, she might have faltered. She'd rather face ten revenue men. "The ladies in this room can no doubt embroider and dance like princesses. But I want to know what *else* they can do."

A held breath, more glances exchanged. Summer grinned, exactly like a twin sister and not very much like the sister of a duke. Especially once such as Callum.

"Three games shall be added," she said, clearly thinking on her feet. Cat liked her instantly. "Archery, swimming, and ..." She paused, clearly trying to think of something else. "And... lawn bowling."

"Lawn bowling!" the dowager duchess exclaimed. "Preposterous. And swimming? Barbaric."

"I'm afraid the duke insisted, Maman," Summer said, still smiling. There was a sharpness to it that Cat understood on a visceral level. Eldest sisters recognized each other, despite titles or breeding. "We cannot have a Cornish duchess who cannot swim. Think of the talk."

As it seemed highly unlikely that the dowager duchess knew how to swim, no one quite knew what to do with their faces. Smile? Nod? Disappearing into the wallpaper with wide eyes seemed to be the current popular choice.

The dowager waved her daughter away, no longer interested.

Viola bounced once on her toes, very, *very* interested. "At least I know I can outswim these fine London ladies."

"As a fisherman's daughter, I should hope so," Cat said. Their father had gone out in weather fair and foul. Until a storm had finally claimed his boat. At seventeen, Matthew barely remembered him. Cat remembered sun-crinkled eyes, hands rough from ropes, and a loud booming laugh.

He'd have hated what Cat had to do to feed their families. Her mother would have applauded her. With the war with France and the inflation of taxes on salt and tea and the half-empty fishing nets, needs must. And it was her mother's connection to a handsome sea captain which allowed it at all. Cat would not squander it.

The dowager let her gaze travel between the debutantes,

snaking between duke's granddaughters and earl's sisters, all the finest the Marriage Mart had to offer. Her face was beautiful, but cold. There would be no quarter given.

"Impress me, ladies."

Cat took a deep breath to calm her roiling stomach. She was thirty years old, for God's sake. She'd faced worse than the *ton*, who would not know her from a hunk of cheese. Which was comforting, actually. Her mother had once brought home three abandoned fox kits who had screamed all night and gave everyone fleas. She'd loved them even when one of them bit her hard enough to require stitches. She still had the scar on her leg. This was nothing.

And regardless, she had no choice. She had to see this through. For the village. For Viola. For Matthew. Both of whom could never, *ever* know about it.

Neither could Callum.

Chapter Two

CAT WAS NOT too proud to make a run for it.

If Callum, the esteemed duke, could do it, so could she.

And what kind of a smuggler would she be if she could not even sneak out of a party? She had once hidden an entire rowboat from a Revenue man.

In the middle of the day.

Twice.

Just for practice.

The parlor was overheated long before the fires of competition whipped through the room—now it could easily double as a new circle of hell. The garden doors beside her were unlocked. No one would notice her absence except for Viola who was right beside her, cheeks pink, brow threatening to perspire. "Hurry," she murmured. "The duchess can't see me sweat."

Luckily, she was too busy assessing the competitors, like a queen at the head of her own personal army. If no one died, this might well become a trend. Cat did not remind her sister that girls from Little Crumpet were unlikely to be on her list for anything other than seat-fillers. She had every confidence Viola would shine.

Just not with sweat, not today.

As the doors were in the presence of the dowager duchess, they were perfectly oiled and did not dare squeak. Success.

Cat stumbled out onto the terrace, blinking in the sudden sunlight, Viola doing the same. The clouds were gathering over the sea, but they had not made it inland yet. They were a bruise on the horizon, boiling and seething with energy. She spared a thought for Matthew, at home with two dogs who hated thunderstorms and two who loved them more than raw beef. The cats, predictably, did not deign to care.

They hurried down the steps into the formal garden. The walkways were swept clean, marching in precise formation between carefully trimmed hedges. There were delicate flowers, marble benches, lazy bumblebees away from the hive. Viola fanned herself. "That was brutal. You must be melting."

Cat nodded. "I'd burn this dress, but I think it might already be on fire."

Their cottage might not be fancy, but it had windows and doors that opened wide to allow for a delicious breeze off the sea. The chimney smoked in winter, but they were used to it. Their mother had pressed shells into the mortar of the windows and hung windchimes made of beach glass from the ceiling. The entire cottage could have fit into the formal drawing room of Penhallow, with room to spare.

The garden paths were wide enough to accommodate a carriage. Viola brushed her hands over the spears of lavender. "Have you noticed? Not a single weed."

The weeds in their vegetable and herb garden were a veritable menace. Sometimes they grew taller than the bean trellis, no matter how often they attacked them. Viola sold watercress bundles when she could, but no one in the village could afford them and most of the time they had to eat their own product or starve. The fishing nets came up emptier and emptier. Two bad summers in a row made for a disaster.

"Clearly they've made a deal with the devil."

"Clearly."

Cat was already feeling more like herself with fresh air in her lungs and a breeze around her ankles. She felt *entirely* like herself when they came across a formal fountain with marble fish and a reclining Poseidon with a perfectly curled beard and a trident in one hand.

And a turtle.

This at least was familiar. Finding animals in odd predicaments was common for the Sparrow family. Their mother had seen to it. It was, in fact, why Cat was going to make such a good smuggler. She was constantly in the oddest places at the oddest times. No one noticed anymore, not even the revenue men. And though new officers had come to town just this past month, they had already been informed by helpful villagers that the eldest Sparrow was odd and not to worry over it. She'd discreetly ordered Guinevere, her largest wolfhound, to jump on an officer with very muddy paws. As a future deterrent. Dog breath was also a most formidable and underestimated weapon.

The turtle was impressively wide and far from home, somehow having found itself inside a stone fountain ornamented with many curlicues that it resembled nothing so much as frozen icing. "Oh, poor thing, he's stuck," Viola said.

The turtle's back was thick and strong, all shades of browns and greens. Cat saw no wounds, no blood clouded the water. "I don't think he's hurt, at least," she said.

"How are we going to get him out of there?"

Cat was wondering the same thing. He was rather wide and cumbersome. Not to mention that snapping turtles were not known to have the softest mouths. Or the kindest dispositions. She touched his shell gently and he eyed her with what could only be called deep distrust. She pushed slightly. He did not so much as budge an inch. "He's absolutely wedged in there. No help for it."

She kicked off her shoes and unrolled her stockings before tying a knot in the bottom of her dress to keep it from dragging. Viola groaned, well used to where this was leading. "Not here. Not *now*," she said. "The dowager duchess could look out the *window*."

"I doubt she can see us from the house," Cat soothed. "And if she can, we'll only look like we're admiring the fountain."

"Or *bathing* in it. They already think us savage."

"And so we are, when required." Cat climbed into the fountain. The water was cool and clean. Poseidon watched her impassively, his crown green with moss. She crouched down, water soaking into her dress despite her precautions. Upon closer inspection, the turtle had wedged itself tightly between two stone whorls. "You're going to have to get in here with me," Cat said.

"Absolutely not. This dress is new! It has silk ribbons!"

"We can't just leave Bartholomew here."

Viola paused. Cat had no doubt that their mother's voice was singing a similar chorus inside her head. "Bartholomew is a ridiculous name." She sighed and scowled at the turtle. "Serves you right. How did you even climb up there?"

He did not deign to reply.

"Sir Bartholomew is a man of mystery," Cat said with a mock sniff.

Viola took her off her shoes with much more care than Cat had shown. Her stockings followed, unmended and pristine. She rolled them carefully and tucked them inside her shoes, far from any offending dirt. Then she sighed again, before stepping up onto the fluted edge of the fountain. She might complain, but she wouldn't leave a creature stuck and stranded any more than Cat would. It just wasn't in their blood.

"At least it's clean," she said, sounding cheerful again. "Remember that pond with the heron stuck in the netting?"

"Remember it?" Cat snorted. "I still have nightmares." It had smelled like rotting death and was full of bugs. The heron, once freed, had left a mess on her arm. Gratitude in the animal kingdom was not particularly clean.

Viola squeezed next to Cat. "This is cozy." Her elbow jabbed Cat's ribs accidentally.

"Ouch."

"Like I said. Cozy."

"Grab the end of the shell there. Mind you don't cut yourself. Ready?" Cat waited for Viola's nod. "One, two… three!"

They pulled.

They pushed.

They heaved to and fro.

Nothing.

Well, not nothing. Bartholomew made a sound very much like a hiss. Cat hadn't known turtles could even make that sound. Could she translate it into English she felt certain it would be more suited to the docks than a duke's gardens. His neck extended and Cat remembered quite suddenly why snapping turtles were called *snapping* turtles.

"Get back!" She shouldered Viola behind her. Viola squeaked.

Bartholomew extended his head again, snapping the air once in warning. Cat stepped back to catch her breath and recalculate their efforts.

"Of course, this couldn't be easy," Viola muttered, wiping water off her face. She pointed at the turtle accusingly. "You, sir, have terrible timing."

As if to prove her point, there was a rustle from the other side of the fountain.

A large man-sized rustle.

Viola peeked over Poseidon's shoulder, staying hidden. She stiffened. "The duke!" Her eyes widened with panic. "Cat, he can't see me like this. It's not *genteel*."

Viola was the only Sparrow with any particular regard for gentility. It did not make her life any easier.

"I'll lose before the games even begin!"

Cat didn't point out that games implied some kind of fun being had and the dowager's competition sounded like anything but. She'd rather sit in this fountain with Bartholomew for the rest of the week.

Viola was confident, kind, competitive. She was also chewing anxiously at her thumbnail. Her breaths were too short, stuttering. Cat tried her most soothing smile. "Vi, it'll be fine. I've got this, you sneak through that juniper hedge and get back to the house."

Viola's mouth trembled. "Truly?"

"Truly. Go."

Viola darted away, relief clear in every line of her body. She didn't care for embarrassment or awkwardness. She liked things in their place. Cat's place was generally in a pond or a cave or up a tree after a cat. Being a Sparrow was not always easy for Viola. Cat was used to it. It did not bother her overmuch. Still, she'd rather not have been caught half-drowned and talking to a turtle inside the duke's very formal stone monstrosity by the duke himself.

His Grace came around the leaping stone dolphins.

Chapter Three

CAT HAD NOT spoken to him in years. She used to see him walking the beach with his pants rolled up. Most undukelike. Most Callum-like. She looked for that familiar walk for weeks, months even, before sternly reminding herself that he was not for the likes of her. Fate had reminded her of that very clearly when he abruptly left for London after his father died. He had stopped talking to her after that. He had stopped talking to everyone. A duke was a duke was a duke, after all.

Trust that same Fate to deliver this as their first proper conversation. With her standing in a pond.

At his marriage tournament.

What if he thought she was here for him?

She was, of course. Just not like that. She wasn't seventeen anymore. She'd given up her infatuation and he had never had one in the first place. She had been a convenient diversion, a stolen kiss. A cliché.

She briefly contemplated hurling herself into the hedges after her sister.

Too late.

Callum stopped very abruptly. No doubt wondering why there was a madwoman in his fountain. "Miss Sparrow. What the hell are you doing?"

She absolutely would not be distracted by the fact that he

remembered her name. Little Crumpet was a small village and no doubt her mother had marched up his driveway to check on the happiness of his horses, dogs, and chickens. More than once. The Sparrow family was not…subtle.

There was no chance that he remembered walking with her along the beach, or that kiss in the tidepool. It was more than ten years ago.

"I've got a turtle," she blurted out.

Nor were the Sparrows particularly eloquent, it seemed.

She was glad, once more, not to be part of the games. If scintillating conversation was on the agenda, she would have already failed.

"He does not appear to appreciate it," Callum remarked.

"Well spotted."

"What are you doing exactly?" His voice was quieter than she remembered, and lower. Threaded through with command. It ghosted pleasantly over the skin. She fervently hoped he would attribute her flushed face to the heat of the day.

"He's stuck."

He just looked at her.

And then he took off his coat.

And his shoes.

"What are you doing?" she asked, sounding far more panicked than was likely warranted.

"I'm freeing a turtle. Before you do yourself an injury and bleed all over the fountain. My mother's aesthetic tastes do not run to the ghoulish." He stepped closer.

She held out a hand, as if she was stopping a goat from headbutting a fence. "But you're a duke!" He'd always been a duke and it had never stopped him before. He'd also been a young man, practically a boy.

Not any longer.

"I assure you I won't melt."

"Neither will I. You should stay over there." *Don't come any closer.* She absolutely did not need to know if he smelled like sandalwood soap or cedar or salt. Or the ocean. He would smell like a storm over the ocean. He always had.

He frowned at her. Folks whispered that he was cold and silent and terrifying, but she had always fancied she saw something else in his brown eyes. A kindness. But that was so many years ago.

Also, his arms were particularly well-muscled, his jaw strong.

It was deeply distracting.

"Be careful, I don't know if he bites," he said, unaware that her thoughts were taking a sharply inappropriate and somewhat salacious turn. His tone was clipped and aristocratic, best suited to beeswax candles and gold plates and duels at dawn.

"He *absolutely* bites," she snorted. She was best suited to beaches and chipped clay plates and a chess piece made from a rutabaga. "That's a snapping turtle. His neck extends further than you think physically possible, after which he will bite your finger clean off."

"Step back," he ordered, even as he immediately stepped closer.

She did no such thing. She wasn't going to let a novice get himself hurt. Especially a *duke*.

"Caitriona," he repeated firmly. She never would have guessed that he might recall her given name. Even if he did sound deeply annoyed. "Now."

She wasn't sure if it was the duke in him or the man in him who issued the quiet command. She absolutely should not like it. She definitely should not obey. On principle, if nothing else. But she already knew she could not manage Bartholomew on her own and being stubborn for the sake of being stubborn was probably not particularly helpful at the moment.

When she stepped up onto the edge, Callum extended his hand to help her. She was very aware of her bare toes and her wet dress brushing her shins. There was no smugness, no arrogance at her acquiescence. Just that stern, unreadable expression. She wondered if there were finishing schools in London just for dukes. If so, they must teach that cold hard glance. There would be awards. Gold ribbons. Callum Winter would be prefect of Duke School.

Even now with his coat hanging from the trident, standing in a fountain with his trousers rolled above his ankles. There was no doubt he held a title. An ancient and venerated one at that. He pushed up his sleeves to reveal strong forearms dusted with hair and tanned from the sun. He looked nothing like a duke.

He looked delicious.

The heat was clearly getting to her. One did not think such thoughts about a duke.

But she very much wanted to lean forward and lick him. Faintly shocked at the way the thought slammed unbidden into her and then proceeded to awaken all sorts of hot tingles, Cat nearly tripped. She had no business wanting to lick him. Especially when her sister was even now preparing to win him like a medieval knight at a tournament winning a prize.

Not to mention that her forthcoming betrayal was a foregone conclusion.

As he was barely acknowledging her presence, she supposed it hardly signified.

Callum looked up suddenly as if she had spoken out loud, dark eyes locking onto her.

"Um," she said. "His name is Bartholomew." *For heaven's sake, Caitriona Sparrow, sort yourself out.*

"Bartholomew."

"Yes. He must have been someone's pet once because he's not native to Britain."

His mouth twitched at her tone. She knew it was sharper than she intended. "And you don't approve," he said.

"I'm sure it was all very sweet for the child who received it, but you shouldn't have a pet if you can't care for it properly."

"I can't argue with that."

People always argued with her over the care of animals. They found her too strict, too blunt. Too messy. He never had though.

Before.

"So, what's to be done then, Miss Sparrow? I am at your pleasure."

Something inside her melted. Or caught fire. She couldn't be sure.

Whatever it was, she was certain it was not *genteel*.

She forced herself not to blush. His gaze was steady, calm. Surely, he hadn't meant the double entendre. He wasn't the sort to tease. Everyone said so.

And yet.

"I need a branch," Cat said, tearing her eyes from him. Naturally, the garden was too well-kept for that. She pulled on a hedge, looking furtively over her shoulder. "Is a gardener likely to get into trouble if I snap this?"

He looked down his very straight nose at her. Why was his nose perfect? "Not from me."

He didn't mention his mother. Neither did she. Instead, she snapped a branch off, making sure it was sturdy.

"Are you going to poke at him?" Callum asked, left eyebrow raising.

"I would never do that. It's just rude." She stepped closer. "I'm going to keep him occupied so that he doesn't take off your hand. Can't have a duke bleeding all over the ladies."

He muttered something about how losing a hand might be worth it if it kept him out of the parlor, the house, and the entirety of Cornwall. She had to grin even if he was not the sort of man who invited grins. "Are you not looking forward to being wooed?"

Now why had she gone and asked that?

He looked as if he was in pain. His sternness intensified, if that was even possible. "If I could hide in this fountain with this turtle, I would."

"That's most unduke-like. And I hear we are to sing for you," she said innocently. It was inappropriate to tease him, but how could she resist, with all his cold dignity?

He narrowed one eye. "And are you going to sing for me, Miss Sparrow?"

Oh my.

"Definitely not."

"Pity."

She snorted. It was safer than examining the warmth that spread through her at his glance, which continued to be somehow stern and reserved, but also searing. She nearly had to search to find her voice. "You wouldn't think so if you'd ever heard me sing."

"I am sure you sing like an angel."

She laughed, ignoring the blandness in his tone which he also somehow managed to make sharp as broken shale. He had definitely ruled Duke School. "Have you ever really paid attention to the biblical description of an angel? Because yes, possibly I sing like a terrifying creature with a thousand eyes, with four faces, on gold wheels."

"And a stick."

She looked down at her hand. "And a stick," she agreed. "Are you ready?"

"You shouldn't—"

"Hush."

Hushing a duke was definitely frowned upon. He looked faintly startled which made her like him that much more, despite herself. He wasn't just a marble statue, he was human. He just looked like a marble statue, with all those hard lines and muscles.

Turtle. Right. Focus on the turtle.

She put the stick near Bartholomew's face and predictably, his neck extended with violent speed. His jaw closed around the offending stick with a powerful snap.

Callum cursed but did not give ground.

"You'd be peevish too if you were stuck here," she merely said, having expected the reaction.

"I *am* stuck here," he muttered. "I'm more concerned with the status of your entire arm. Stand back now."

"I'm perfectly well," she assured him surely. "This is not my first time." And didn't *that* sound entirely too suggestive? She stared at the turtle, refusing to look up at Callum even though she felt the weight of his gaze on her. Was there something in the fountain's water? She felt nearly tipsy.

"His jaws are locked in." she finally added. "You could move him now, I think." Bartholomew glared at her. "You have very bad manners, sir," she informed him.

Callum reached down to grip the shell. It was slippery, hard work and Cat knew exactly how rough and unforgiving the edges of a turtle's shell could be. His forearms flexed. Bartholomew's eyes rolled slightly, and his jaws moved. He was definitely peeved. "We're trying to help you," Cat scolded. "Don't be so ungrateful."

"Miss Sparrow, if he releases that stick, you are to get out of the way immediately."

She waved a hand dismissively "Yes, yes." She lifted an eyebrow. "You should pull harder."

"Is that what I should do?" he asked, softly, dryly.

"Better yet, if you push down on the edge there, he should pop free." She leaned closer to better point out the spot. "Just here—"

"Caitriona, don't." His voice was a controlled lash. Expecting to be obeyed. And he'd said her name again. She wasn't a silly schoolgirl to be offended. Especially not when she liked it so much. The way he rolled the syllables in his mouth, it sounded like the wind off the moors, the sea finding its way home. She felt it everywhere.

He shifted his stance.

The shell released.

Without warning.

Bartholomew shot over the lip of the fountain. Time slowed down, stopped. Water droplets sparkled near Cat's nose. He finally landed safely on a patch of grass. Then he trundled off without so much as a how-do-you-do.

Or an apology.

Because his sudden freedom also came with a certain amount of momentum. Enough to cause Callum to stagger. He slid and lost his balance, falling into the water with a resounding and impressive splash. Cat jerked to the side to avoid being smacked in the face with a turtle-projectile, stumbled against the stone edge, floundered, and fell right in next to him. With a yelp. And a splash to rival Callum's own.

All in all, not her most graceful moment.

Callum pushed out of the water that fell directly into his face from a carved conch shell and tossed his hair back. He reached for Cat who coughed and choked. "Are you hurt? Caitriona, answer me, are you—"

She wasn't choking on fountain water.

Well, not *only* fountain water.

Mostly laughter. Callum paused. It only made her laugh harder. His answering smile was slow, nearly shy and it transformed his entire face. He was still somberly handsome, with that quiet intensity, but now there was a sweetness to him.

She had a sudden, intense craving for dessert.

The smile vanished so quickly she might have imagined it.

She hadn't though. And the need to make him smile again tingled inside her chest.

She was never going to be a duchess, but sitting in a fountain with a duke while a rescued turtle sauntered away was far more fitting for someone like her. More amusing, too, it had to be said. Even if her dress now weighed as much as a house. It tangled around her knees as she tried to clamber out.

Callum stood and offered his hand again, dripping water from hair gone dark and tangled. The thin lawn of his shirt molded to his chest, outlining his muscles. Even soaked through, he exuded the bearing of an aristocrat. His back was straight, his expression calm.

Until a tiny frog plopped out of a fold of his shirt.

She guffawed. She wished she could say it had been a demure

giggle, a seductive chuckle. But alas, a guffaw.

She pulled the wet mass of her dress out the fountain, guffaw giving way to a chortle. Not precisely an improvement. "If only turtle-dodging were a contest, I'd fancy myself the winner."

"It might be better than what my mother has planned." No smile this time, but a gleam of amusement; something to be shared between them.

Oh, she could be in trouble with this man.

Again.

And she could not afford to be. She could not forget why she was here. What she must do.

To him.

"Let me escort you back to the house," he said.

"I hear the ladies in London dampen their dresses," she said, water squelching with every step as they moved through the garden. "I can't say I see the appeal."

He glanced down at her, glanced away, all while making a sound in the back of his throat, a kind of hum that somehow touched the back of her thighs.

Before she could consider it more closely, a gasp sounded from inside an open door. Heads turned as one, glasses stilled, still touching lips. "Bollocks," Callum said under his breath. "I assumed they'd still be in the main parlor."

The guests had begun a tour of the house, admiring paintings and marble floors and silk wallpaper. Not to mention a very damp duke and a woman soaked through and with hair that no doubt had not been improved by the attention. It clung like seaweed to the side of her neck. "We should have taken the kitchen door," Cat whispered.

"I would not insult your dignity," Callum said, without an ounce of irony.

"Dignity is overrated." There were at least six women and three men within direct eyesight who had noticed their closeness, the air of a shared moment, and might now cheerfully strangle her before dinner.

Behind them, Viola darted towards the stairs, slippers in hand. She looked like a beautiful selkie in search of her sealskin. Cat was fairly certain *she* looked like Jenny Greenteeth, haunting the waterways in search of children to steal. She would have known it even without the shocked glares currently being hurled in her direction.

"I'd rather face ten snapping turtles," Callum muttered.

"You're not the one they are going to bite."

He looked down at her. "They aren't going to bite you either," he said, dark and low. "I can promise you that."

Chapter Four

"WELL, I AM quite sure you made an impression," Viola chortled an hour later as she finished pinning up her hair. "Mother always said it was better to be odd than forgettable."

"I'm not sure this is what she meant."

"It's exactly what she meant, and you know it."

Fair point. Their mother would have loved hearing every ridiculous second of the story, once she'd been assured of the safety of the turtle, of course. Cat did not mention the way Callum had made her feel, standing in his shirtsleeves. Looking at her so directly. At thirty, she was accustomed to not being looked at all or else expected to swoon with gratitude for a mere glance. But Callum had not only looked at her, he had made her feel *seen*.

In just a few minutes, and with a peevish turtle between them. Even if she wasn't confident that he liked what he saw.

He was clearly very, very dangerous.

She resolved to stop thinking about him. He might one day be her brother-in-law. Worse, if she followed through with her plans, he would hate her.

When she followed through with her plans.

She had no choice. Not if she wanted to keep a roof, however crooked and leaky, over their heads. Not if she wanted to keep the cottage with its secret slipway to the beach and its surprisingly large cellar. She had her siblings to look after, not to mention a menagerie of creatures great and small. And a village teetering on the brink of disaster.

Never mind the threat of being deported to Australia.

Or hanged.

Her brother already went out with the fishing boats more often than she liked. Between the storms, the rival smugglers, and the French, it was dangerous work. He already looked so much like their father. And fishing wasn't what called to him. He'd rather be a blacksmith and though Arthur, the village smith, had showed him what he could, neither could afford a proper apprenticeship. Yet.

She'd find a way.

Somehow.

And a duke could survive anything. A spinster in Little Crumpet with very few coins to her name was another matter altogether. If she stumbled, there was no one to catch her. Or her family. Everyone in the village were in similar straits.

The duke wouldn't know a strait if it bit him on his very perfect nose.

With the reminder doing little to mitigate the sour burning in her belly, Cat turned back to her sister with a forced smile. This was supposed to be a holiday for Viola. A chance at a different life, even if she herself did not see the appeal. To be fair, she saw the appeal of a full belly and never having to clean a chamber pot again, but she did not see the appeal of living in London and choking on coal smoke. Not when you could live by the sea with its pink sunsets and wild storms.

"I suppose my dramatic entrance hardly signifies," she said lightly. "As I am not competing. Hopefully, I haven't damaged *your* chances though."

"As if I would ever marry a man who was not kind to you," Viola said, pulling a curl from her chignon to lay over her shoulder. It made her look as delicate as a cameo. A tiny pearl lay between her collarbones. She'd found it herself one night over a supper of oysters and clams in fish broth. Matthew had carefully pushed a needle through it over the course of the next day and Cat had found a gold ribbon in her mother's memory box. They'd put it together as a present for Viola's twentieth birthday and she'd barely taken it off since.

"Anyway," she added, turning away from the looking glass. "You saved me. Thank you, Cat."

Cat waved it away. "What are big sisters for?"

"Wrestling turtles?"

"Exactly."

"Well, the duke did not look displeased with you, from my quick glimpse of him. Well, not any *more* displeased than usual, anyway. He does have a fearsome countenance. Only he's rather handsome and I'm not sure anyone notices. Or I suppose they must, it's only that it makes no matter to them. Not with his other attributes."

Viola had been barely eleven when Cat found herself thoroughly infatuated by Callum. And then forgotten. Her mother had called her a fool. Dukes were dukes. Girls from fishing villages remained girls from fishing villages.

"The duchess on the other hand…" Viola made a face. "I think God Himself would only receive a disdainful sniff."

"Yes." Cat grinned. "And I wish you the best of luck with your future mother-in-law."

"Beast." Viola adjusted her long gloves and passed a pair to Cat. They were a bright peony-pink, stunning as a sunset. "Here."

"Those are your favorite."

"And they will look stunning with your dress." Cat wore a dove-gray gown, cobbled together from her one mourning gown, now three years out of date. "I know we can only afford half a wardrobe as it is," Viola added. "But it's no reason for you to be stuck in plain colors."

"I don't mind." They generally hid dog fur better anyway. And yellow dresses were rather noticeable in the caves at midnight.

"Well, I do. You are every bit as pretty as anyone down there, and I mean to make sure every gentleman downstairs notices it."

Cat laughed. "Then I really will be murdered before dessert. We should hurry, we're already late as it is." The dinner bell had rung fifteen minutes ago.

"And everyone *else* will be early," Viola said smugly. "I mean to stand out."

Cat hugged her briefly. "I am quite sure I've exalted the Sparrow name quite enough for one day, but I bow to your wisdom."

The clock struck eight.

"What is it?" Viola asked over her shoulder when Cat did not follow her to the door of their shared sitting room.

"My stocking ribbon has come loose," she fibbed. "I'll be down presently."

"I can wait for you."

"No, no," Cat hoped her smile was more natural than it felt. "Go make your entrance."

Cat waited until her sister was gone. Her stockings, not made of the finest silk, were perfectly secure.

Her heart thumped in her chest as she pushed inside to her bedroom. Her book was where she had left it on the window seat. The green chair embroidered with little birds was still angled by the fireplace next to the table with lion paws for legs. The wardrobe was undisturbed. Her wet chemise from this afternoon hung over the screen in the corner.

But on her pillow lay a single iron key.

Her pulse doubled, thrumming in her ears. She had paid a small fortune to one of the housemaids for this key.

It was, quite literally, the key to her future.

Chapter Five

N O ONE PAID Cat much mind when she slipped into the drawing room. Heads turned in her direction and turned away again, uninterested. No titles or wealth to be had from her and therefore not enough to tempt anyone away from waiting for a duke. She was grateful for it as it gave her another moment to gather her composure. If Viola thought something was afoot, she would hound her day and night. And if she couldn't fool her sister, how could she fool the revenue men?

If this had been a usual day she would have risen at dawn, wandered down to the rocky beach with a sweet roll and an apple and her dogs: King Arthur, Merlin, Percival and Guinevere. She would have fed the ducks who gathered behind the inn, greeted Arthur stoking the forge's fire. Several cats, birds and stray dogs would have followed her through the streets, waiting for treats, which she always provided. Granny Goodwin would have been sitting out on her stoop with her corncob pipe, feeding her crows. She would have a piece of advice or gossip, a saucy wink if the baker's eldest son walked up from the beach without his shirt.

Cat would have returned home to make breakfast for Viola and Matthew, followed by the feeding of rabbits, hedgehogs, more cats and dogs, and Mordred, the one-eyed fox who liked to sleep behind her cabbages. There'd be the garden to care for, bread to be baked. During the summer months Viola sometimes acted as a lady's companion to those traveling to the seaside for a rest.

She'd have gone by the caves, checked the stone where notes were left by Captain Davignon coming in from the Channel Islands and France with contraband. After her father had died, Cat's mother had met the captain while she was visiting St. Ives and he was offloading brandy. Their affair was sporadic at best, but it lasted many years. He had often sent scraps of lace to Cat and Viola, and had sent Matthew's first jug of brandy, which he drank in one sitting and cursed for the rest of the year.

Cat would need a gang to move the cargo once it dropped, batmen to protect them, several places to hide the lace and the brandy, someone to transport it, someone to sell it discretely. Captain Davignon could provide her with goods, but not men.

And so: an extravagant house party. Access to the kind of society she would never have had otherwise, people who might have their eye caught by fine French lace, who might bemoan the lack of brandy, the price of tea. Society folk who shopped as if it was air. A merchant in Bristol or London would not give Cat the time of day, but they'd bend over backwards for an aristocrat.

Which brought her here with fine contraband lace stitched to her neckline in the hopes that it might pique interest. She would unstitch it tonight and add it to the next dress. The official story was that Viola had made it herself, but Cat figured she could gauge from there who might be worth approaching.

All to say she had not counted on a duke sitting in a fountain, and a turtle. And now, formal gowns, talk of the weather, held breaths waiting for that same duke to arrive. A key hidden in her stays, burning like a hot coal. It felt obvious, as if smoke billowed from the lace at her neckline. She shifted.

The King himself might have been in attendance by the way the guests scrambled to be the first to bow or curtsy when Callum finally arrived. He did look rather regal for someone who had spent a considerable amount of time wrestling an ungrateful snapping turtle. He wore a burgundy waistcoat, and a black coat with gold buttons. His pocket watch gleamed gold, as did the pin in his simple cravat. This was a man who did not have to pretend, or impress. It was bred into his blood. And he knew it, made no apologies for it.

Or for his disinterest even as the windowpanes shook with the force of so many murmurs of "Your Grace".

Callum looked calm, if stark. The more he let the chatter break against the boulder of his silence, the more it increased in frenzy. Why did she fancy she could see him glance in her direction, a softening of those stark eyebrows? She would have understood every minute shift in his expression once. During that one brief summer.

Cat was surprised when Viola joined her. "Aren't you going to enter the fray?"

"Certainly not," she said, accepting a flute of champagne instead. "I will not be herded."

"What if someone else catches his eye?" Cat asked, pretending the thought did not make her feel odd in a hundred miserable ways.

"He's overrun," Viola explained. "Much like the cabbage patch that summer Mother refused to let us fight back against the rabbits, do you remember?"

Their mother loved rabbits almost as much as rabbits loved her cabbage patch.

"And the duke is a cabbage in this scenario?"

Viola winked, careful to hide it from the others. Winking was not done by young ladies, and the battle had clearly begun. She nodded at another lady who hovered by the window, the gold brocade draperies perfectly setting off the red of her dress. Her hooded eyes were as black as her hair shining and straight as a pin. "Now *she* is a contender," Viola said. "Lady Ruby Chatsworth knows how to hold attention. She'll be one to watch."

"You're quite right," Lady Summer interjected cheerfully from behind them. She wore butter-yellow and was crowned with yellow roses. They glowed against her rich brown curls. She was not identical to Callum but there were similarities in their smiles, the arch of their brows. But Summer was all insouciance against Callum's seriousness.

"Lady Summer!" Cat and Viola offered a flurry of slightly flustered curtsies.

"My brother is not a cabbage though," she corrected, grinning. "More like a turnip."

Cat and Viola froze. Calling a duke a cabbage in his own house, never mind to his sister, was bad enough. Any comparison to vegetables was probably frowned upon. They might not be Quality, but it was a safe enough guess.

The Sparrow family really was too feral for these kinds of parties.

But as Cat had thought earlier, sisters recognized sisters. Cat and Viola exchanged a glance. The temptation to call Matthew a turnip was sometimes overwhelming.

Summer pounced on it. "You must have a brother."

"We do," Cat admitted. "Definitely a turnip."

Summer laughed. It was loud and joyful and snared smiles form the other guests.

"Your ladyship is very kind to greet us personally," Viola said, remembering her manners.

"Oh don't," Summer pleaded. "I've been fussed at by two dozen ladies already and if you have a brother then you must know that I cannot tell him what to do and so any kind of flattery is wasted on me."

Viola raised her eyebrows. "But can you doctor the competition?"

"I can but I won't," Summer replied, much of her natural warmth fading. The resemblance to her brother increased. She suddenly had the sharpness of a knight on the eve of battle rather than a lady in silk.

"Good," Viola twinkled over the rim of her glass, unperturbed. "It will be so much more rewarding when I trounce everyone here *without* cheating."

Summer paused, then grinned. "Oh, I *knew* I liked you." She tilted her head in Cat's direction. "Are you recovered from your afternoon?"

"Perfectly," Cat assured her. "It's hardly the first time I've toppled headfirst into water after an animal and I'm sure it won't be the last."

"I am glad to know you are made of sturdy stuff. And will you compete with your sister?"

"For a man?" Cat asked, forgetting to play coy or to fuss with words as she ought to. "Absolutely not." No matter how much Callum invaded her thoughts. "But for the last currant bun? To the death." She hadn't had one since last Christmas. Sometimes she dreamt about them.

"She's vicious," Viola agreed.

"I shall keep that in mind," Summer laughed.

Callum had just made it through the bejeweled mob when the butler announced a tardy guest. "Lord Eliot Howard, the Earl of Blackpool."

Summer groaned. "Bollocks." She gave Cat a sidelong glance. "Forget I said that."

"Forget what? I must have gotten water in my ear today and I cannot hear very well out of that side."

Summer slipped her arm through Cat's as though they were already lifelong friends. There were tiny glass beads stitched to her gloves. They could keep a family in flour and bacon for a month. "Are you quite sure you won't compete for my brother?"

Cat thought of his strong, gentle hands. His brief, shy smile like candlelight in a winter window. The key lodged behind the bones of her stays dug into her skin.

"Alas," she replied, keeping her tone light.

"It's on you then, Miss Viola," Summer said.

"I'm ready."

"I am happy to hear it," she said, as her mother was announced by the butler. "Because here we go."

"I thought it was to start tomorrow?" Viola asked, already

putting her glass down in anticipation. She would have rubbed her hands with glee if she thought no one was watching.

"Don't be fooled," Summer murmured. "It started the very moment the invitations were issued."

Cat had paid dearly for their invitation.

Naturally, she did not say so.

The dowager duchess surveyed the acolytes, staring down her patrician nose. The woman did not appear to blink. It was unnerving. Her dress was the color of ice, the kind that broke under you on a pond in later winter with no warning. Equally unnerving.

A hush fell and she took it as her due. "A duchess knows her curtsies."

There was a pause, a shiver of understanding, and then a veritable stampede.

Callum moved as if to slip out, but his mother's hand caught him, nails digging into his sleeve. He allowed it. Cat imagined he did not wish to cause a further scene. As if that were even possible. His gaze settled on her. She could not read it.

Hopeful duchesses-to-be approached the dowager. Candlelight gleamed off gold and silk and jewels. It was as bad as making your curtsy to the queen. Or so Cat imagined. Women from fishing villages were not invited to the palace. But at eleven, Viola had decided it was quite possible that the queen might come to Cornwall for stargazy pie, and so she rigorously practiced her curtsies. Truly, there were princesses with less practice. Their mother forced her to stop when her left knee swelled up in protest.

"It's ghastly, isn't it?" Summer said. "I can't imagine what my mother is thinking."

"And your brother?" She should not have asked. It was too forward.

"This was not Callum's idea, I assure you. I can't think why he allows it."

Callum's expression did not change. He was silent and his

reputation for being cold and imposing solidified, especially next to Lord Blackpool who leaned against the wall next to him with a smile or a wink for every lady. They approached the dowager duchess flustered and left, just as flustered, if for another reason. The earl was very handsome with straight dark hair from his French-Micmac mother. He drew the eye and knew it well. But Cat's eye still skipped over him entirely. Lord Blackpool was fairy glitter. Callum's presence had weight. She felt it like a hand gripping her throat. His hand.

She could see it clearly and wondered how everyone else only saw that terrifying severity. A flash of the Callum she had once known superimposed over this older, perfect version.

"Lady Ruby's curtsy is flawless," Summer murmured. "Lady Imogen is lovely, but her father is political. He would marry her to a goat if he thought it would further his ambitions."

"And that matters?"

"It will when he pressures her too hard, and she cracks." Summer tilted her head. "Lady Siddal is a widow, but penniless. She may be ruthless."

Cat snorted. Lady Siddal hadn't met Viola.

They watched as her sister was the last to reach the dowager. Any order of precedence would put her there due to rank. She might be expected to show embarrassment or self-deprecation. Viola, instead, used it as the perfect frame to a piece of unexpected but beautiful art. She had everyone's attention.

Why then, was Callum looking at Cat?

Cat tried not to look back.

Viola curtsied, graceful, elegant. Not too ostentatious, not so simple as to be found wanting. Cat had not realized just how loudly a curtsy could speak.

The dowager duchess narrowed her eyes.

And then she inclined her head.

Impressed.

Chapter Six

CALLUM WINTER, THE eleventh Duke of Tremaine, had launched a turtle at a lady's head.

At *Caitriona Sparrow's* head.

He might not have Blackpool's easy manners, but even he knew better than to toss animals at ladies or those same ladies into fountains. Usually, he had exquisite control of his expression. His every movement. It had come at some cost.

Cat hadn't screamed or swooned or used it as an excuse to have him carry her inside in his arms.

Pity on that last part.

She'd only laughed and trudged through the pristine garden smelling like water and mint. Her dress had clung to her, holding her curves the way he knew he would dream of holding them tonight. She would be warm and soft. Smiling. He'd seen her real smile today and now nothing else would do.

It had been too long.

Too many desperate years pretending not to watch her walk the beach the few times he had returned. Pretending not to wait to see her walk past with her dogs, laughing when they pulled her into a run.

Pretending, pretending.

He was very, very good at it.

Honestly, he was suddenly feeling very fond of Bartholomew.

It was the longest he'd spent in Caitriona's company.

And goddamn it, that wet dress.

If he ever found that turtle, he might have a tiny, jeweled crown made. Or a dashing cape. Something to commemorate services to a duke.

He shifted. Best not to think of that wet dress. Not when he was under the kind of scrutiny that frankly made his balls want to shrivel up. Only thoughts of Caitriona Sparrow could compete. And long years of assuming a certain kind of dignity under the watchful eye of his mother, of the House of Lords, of the prince himself.

Speaking of competition.

It was too much to hope that she might be here for these blasted games. His mother would only have invited a village girl to pad the numbers or to exhibit noble munificence. Or, even more likely, she thought showcasing sophisticated titled ladies of quality against women from a fishing village would sway him.

And it absolutely did.

Though obviously in the very opposite direction his mother intended.

Nobody could hold a candle to Caitriona. They never could.

Hardly a surprise his mother did not realize that. She did not know him at all. A fact that continued to vex her. She ought to know him because he ought to be her creature: a perfect duke.

He had been. For a little while.

But they both knew he wasn't anymore and hadn't been for a long time. Not where it counted. He fought too many of the old guard in Parliament, agitated for change in the cold sharp voice he had perfected. Wielded shame and disdain like a cudgel. Just as he'd been taught.

A duke definitely did not hide in the upper family parlor. It was the safest place in the house and always had been. His mother would ride a pig to market before she set foot in this little room. It smelled of damp, and when the wind came in at just the perfect angle, fish. He'd known it at age three, and he knew it at age thirty-three. No one would ever think to look for him here.

Except his twin sister Summer.

After all, she was the one who had hidden the fish, all those years ago.

"There you are," she said, popping through the door. Her brown hair curled around her face, escaping pins. The heat of the long day was beginning to intrude. "You're late. They're waiting for you."

She could have been referencing the French army instead of an army of debutantes. His reaction was the same, right down to the needles in his stomach. He scrubbed his face. It had been so quiet to walk the cliffs alone this morning and climb down to the beach to watch the sun on the water. He always missed Cornwall when he was away, and he was always away. He considered stealing a fishing boat and not returning until next month sometime. Only the thought of leaving his sister alone with their mother gave him pause. Summer was not above pushing their exacting, critical mother right into the ornamental pond. Gleefully.

"Tell me again why I'm allowing this?" he groaned, turning back to stare outside the window. The guests milled on the flagstones below, whispering behind their fans or their champagne. Casting glances at the house, as if they knew where he was.

"Our mother is the devil herself," Summer pointed out. "Also, she wasn't exactly forthcoming with the plan."

The dowager duchess, London-born but married to the Cornish duke at sixteen, preferred to stay in London. She did not appreciate what the sea winds did to her hair. Or the lack of Society. The smell of salt and seaweed and fish. The exact same things Callum loved best about living in Cornwall, between the wild ocean and the moors. They had seven country estates, three London houses, and a townhouse in Edinburgh, but Penhallow would always be home.

Because of Cat.

His mother felt very differently. Always had. And so there was no warning, not even a tingle of premonition before her carriage pulled up followed by seven more carriages stuffed with all the necessities one might need on hand for a country house party, along with her London staff because London servants had more panache.

"She can't be serious," he said, feeling a cold wash of fear, the same as the night he'd been caught unawares by a storm and tossed from the rowboat into the churning waters. His mother was not just hunting for the next duchess, she was *auditioning her.*

And he was sneaking off to wrestle a turtle with Caitriona. He'd take that any day.

"I'm afraid she is very serious. Though she's more interested in finding herself the perfect daughter-in-law than you a wife."

"I suppose that's hardly a surprise."

She wrinkled her nose. "She has abandoned subtlety altogether. I did what I could. Not that I think archery or swimming prowess will make much of a difference either way. But I couldn't just let it stand. As your sister, and as a woman, frankly."

Growing up, Callum was informed on a daily basis that dukes did not shout. Nor did they crouch to pull kittens out of a haybale, laugh, yawn, or itch. He'd also been assured that he would never be *forced* to shout since dukes were generally obeyed by everyone but the king and God. Except for his mother, of course.

Or his sister, come to think of it.

He kept his voice very, very even out of long habit. Any inflection that might suggest temper or emotion had been roundly scorned since he was in short pants. And as he grew older every twitch of his face was scrutinized. Was he flirting? Was he impressed? Might he be amenable to an alliance? To sign a Bill for Parliament? Offer marriage? Would he pay off the gambling debts of his cousin's mother-in-law? Or his own cousin Graham's for that matter, which always exceeded the debt of a small country. He was currently heir to the Tremaine title and already considered it his due.

"Maybe it won't be so bad," Summer said.

He stared at her blankly for a full minute. She had clearly landed on her head in the last ten minutes. It came as no surprise that his mother, and in fact all of Society, expected him to marry. A duke must…well…*duke*. Running several estates and taking his seat in Parliament was expected and done mostly without complaint. Marrying in order to sire an heir was another matter entirely. He had nothing against marriage or babies. Nothing against women, either.

But if he could not marry Cat, what was the point?

And it just seemed a forced business all around, since Graham would inherit the title and everything that went with it when he died. He was a Winter, so the Tremaine duchy would stay in the family. Despite what his mother had to say about it. And Summer. It was the only thing they agreed on.

Graham was not a favorite.

To put it mildly.

And it was the only reason why Summer would even *consider* acquiescing to his mother's plans. "This is about Graham, isn't it?"

Summer hissed. There was no other word for it. And he knew she would have spat right on the ground at the mention of his name if there weren't servants rushing to and fro in the hallway. "You're not going to die and leave him as my guardian."

"Summer, you're thirty-three years old. You hardly need a guardian."

"Bringing my age into it," she muttered, narrowing one eye in a clear threat to his health and happiness. "Are you choosing violence, little brother?" He snorted. She tossed her hair back in a way that could only be described as autocratic. "I want my future nephew to inherit. Not that lecher."

"Fair enough. But I, on the other hand, don't particularly care who inherits."

"As they inherit *me* as well, you *should* care." She kicked him with the toe of her shoe. And not particularly gently. "You should care desperately."

"You will be your husband's problem, surely, when I die."

She scoffed. "You must be joking." It was no secret that she had no intention of marrying. Her affairs were discreet, for the most part, and so did not attract much gossip. Not to mention that she was far outside the age of a debutante, and was a sister to a duke who did not tolerate any contempt towards his twin. "No cage for me, little brother. But we must take control of this little fiasco."

She tapped her lip, clearly thinking dark thoughts. "Anyway, you owe me," she sniffed. "I'm six minutes older than you are and I should have been the duke. I'd make a grand duke."

"You would," he agreed. Dukes were meant to be charming and ruthlessly confident. They weren't meant to prefer the sound of the ocean to the pianoforte or fish fried on the beach to lobster in bechamel sauce served on silver plates. Not that Callum had admitted it to anyone but Summer. Their mother's standards were military and nearly biblical. In fact, she'd written a tome on etiquette that was twice the length of the family Bible. The illustrated one with the family tree. "But that's not how primogeniture works, and you know it."

"Still, you stole my inheritance. You can do this one little thing for me."

"Get married?"

"Use this horrendous opportunity to our advantage."

Her pout did not move him. "You said the very same on our eighth birthday when you wanted my horse." According to their mother dukes rode thoroughbreds, and it was never too early to learn. Duke's sisters, however, rode a fat old pony who preferred eating grass to almost anything else. Callum had loved that pony. His horse, on the other hand, tossed him to the ground weekly. "And the next year when you needed an alibi after stealing mother's pearls and losing them." *Losing* was a bit of a stretch. She'd flung each pearl into the ocean in an effort to bribe a mermaid to show herself. "And just last week when you wanted the last treacle tart," he pointed out.

She shrugged one shoulder, grinning. "Heavy is the head that bears the ducal crown, Cal."

"Dukes don't wear crowns."

"I would definitely have a crown were I duke. At the very least, a disgustingly ostentatious tiara."

"You have seven of those, at last count." And she could buy seven hundred more. He wasn't the least bit fussed over it.

"Wasted on you. Utterly."

"True."

"We can't stop this," she said, softly. "But we can alter it."

"I don't give a damn about curtsies and swimming prowess."

His mother meant to choose a duchess for her social qualities, for talents such as embroidery, music, French, watercolors, dancing. Embarrassing the family name would not be tolerated. It never had been. Not even when he was in leading strings and barely even knew how to say the word duke. He had been in lessons since before he could walk: how to talk, how to walk, how to fence, ride a horse, wear a coat.

So a competition. For his hand in marriage.

To a woman who knew how to do all of those things. How to curtsy and host dinners and speak French and Italian, but only to flatter.

Like hell.

What he wanted was Caitriona's laugh when a turtle sailed past her.

"Miss Viola Sparrow is worth a second look. I am quite certain she will be seated next to you tomorrow at dinner. Her curtsy was impeccable."

He hadn't even noticed. He'd been too distracted by Caitriona.

"She's a girl."

"She's twenty-three. Twenty-four? She *is* on the shelf, but she's lovely. They all are." Something sharpened in her gaze, then faded. "You danced with her at the Spring Fair, remember?"

He remembered. She *was* lovely. But young. "Summer, I'm too old for her."

"Pish."

"Then she's too young for me."

"She's nice."

"I didn't say she wasn't nice."

She just wasn't Cat.

He might not have had many opportunities to speak to Caitriona since that brief summer before his father died, but he recalled every interaction. Vividly. The way the sun burned red in her dark hair, her easy smile. The fact that she always had mud on her boots or dog fur on her hem. Simple things that should not draw him to her but did. Every single time. Duchess material or not.

Not that she would notice. He made very sure of that. Too many eyes tracked his every movement, his every expression when he went into public. It was safer to hide it all behind the icy ducal façade of a Tremaine.

She was reason enough to stay and see this farce through. How else was he to spend any time with her?

Perhaps Summer was right, after all. This could be a blessing in disguise.

"May as well cross Miss Lewis off the list too, then," Summer said. "She's only just turned twenty."

He shuddered.

Caitriona was a woman, not a girl. She had curves and confidence. She looked a man in the eye. And she'd never once giggled to placate him. Not that he would mind if she did—and not that he would ever say so.

Summer patted his arm, misreading his expression. "I know it's gruesome, but I really do think it might be good for you. I just want you to be happy, Callum."

He blinked, bewildered. "I am happy. Well, I *was*. Before today."

"*Happier* then."

"I'm hardly the sort to dance a jig either way, Summer."

"I suppose. And it's not the material point, is it?"

"What is, then?"

"Caitriona Sparrow," Summer informed him smugly.

Callum froze. "Don't."

She scowled at him. "*You* don't. I'm not blind, you idiot. Not now and not when we were younger."

"Summer."

"I like her."

He scrubbed a hand over his face.

"And I know you like her too."

He nearly snorted. *Like* was such an insipid word. One liked tea with lemon. Gothic novels. Warm blankets in winter. What he felt for Caitriona was both desperate and steadying. Unyielding. And it went deeper, so much deeper. Craving. Worship. *Need*.

One didn't *like* breathing. It was simply a necessity.

Summer dropped the subject, but he knew it was only a momentary reprieve. She was as relentless as their mother, in her own way. "Well, at the very least this will be so much more fun than the usual sneak attacks by matchmaking mamas and desperate papas."

"Fun for *you*."

"Well, naturally. But I mean to fix this for you, Callum. Leave it to me, little brother. I have a feeling about this."

"I swear the devil himself just shuddered."

"The devil is nothing," Summer scoffed, a hard gleam in her eye. "I mean to take on Maman. And I mean to win."

"You always do," Blackpool interrupted with a smirk, suddenly leaning in the doorway. He smiled his crooked smile in Summer's direction.

She scowled, as expected. "What are you doing here?"

"I was invited."

She sniffed.

"What is going on out there?" Summer might be immune, but he was as fashionable as ever, with tousled hair and a smile that generally made women sigh, age three to a hundred and three. Callum had never learned the trick of it. There was always too much riding on every minute detail of his smile, his frown. The way his left eyelid twitched when he was tired. "It's brutal down there. Like being thrown into bloody waters for the shark's pleasure."

"Mother." Callum tossed back the rest of his champagne. It was too dry, too sharp. Too obvious. He set the glass on the windowsill.

"Ah. Of course." He raised his eyebrows. "Am I to be your loyal squire then?"

Callum snorted. "You can be the damn knight in shining armor."

"I usually am, old man."

A fact that Callum never resented. He appreciated it deeply. Eliot caught attention and held it effortlessly. He enjoyed the nuances, the words behind the words in a way Callum never could. He was fairly certain he had survived school relatively unscathed solely because of Eliot. He softened everyone around him. There were few people Callum could trust at the end of the day.

"Oh, please," Summer muttered. He also never failed to get a rise out of her.

"So what's the occasion? I know I've just arrived from the wilds of Wales but that was an awful lot of curtsying, even for your illustrious Maman."

Callum mumbled.

"What's that?" Eliot pressed.

Callum sighed. He may as well get it over with. "Mother has decided to hold a competition."

"For what?"

"To find me a wife."

"Not only that," Summer added. "She made it public

knowledge in London." She waved a folded gossip newspaper in her hand. He hadn't noticed it before. Brooding took concentration. "They are calling it The Duchess Games."

It took a full three minutes for Blackpool to stop laughing.

Friend or not, it wasn't to say that the man wasn't also an ass.

Chapter Seven

SNEAKING OUT OF a fancy house in the middle of the night proved more difficult than Cat would have guessed.

For one thing, she nearly ran into several ladies and two gentlemen, all furtively darting towards bedrooms not their own. None of them had headed towards the family wing. Towards Callum's bedroom. A matter which was none of her business and about which she should not care. Did not care.

Absolutely cared.

Blast.

Get your head in the game, Cat. Smugglers whose minds wandered were not smugglers for long.

She dodged clandestine lovers, a footman posted by the front door overnight, and the light from several lamps left burning for the comfort of guests in a palatial house that was not their own. She climbed out a window in a music room tucked in the back corner which deposited her conveniently between two juniper hedges. She made her way through the gardens by the moon, not daring to light a lantern until she was safely out of sight.

She was not far from home and stopped to fetch one of the dogs. Percival, one of the wolfhound puppies, nearly knocked her down in his haste to show his joy that she had returned from her long travels abroad. His enormous paws slammed onto her shoulders so he could lick the side of her face in case she had any doubts to his faithfulness. She may as well have been away for a month, not a single day. She laughed, momentarily robbed of her worries. But in the end, she took King Arthur along with her. He might not be as large as the wolfhounds, but his black fur easily faded into the shadows, and he was old enough to know what he was about.

Her brother was not in his bed, and she would not ask where he was or with whom. They had decided long ago that the cottage was a safe haven. A place to be entirely oneself. No judgment, no pretenses.

She had also decided, long ago, that he would never be part of the village smuggling operation. Matthew was bright and kind but a terrible liar. And young. Viola was so pretty that while other villages were told to "watch the wall" when smugglers went by with their haul, Viola was called out to flirt. Revenue men watched Viola. But it was dangerous, imperfect work. Viola deserved so much better.

But Cat—Cat was a strong sturdy woman who could wrestle the waves and haul a crate. She could read and write and keep accounts. She could walk anywhere at any time with her collection of dogs with no one the wiser.

And she lived in a cottage with perfect access.

She climbed down the hidden slipway, King Arthur at her heels and the sound of the waves as a welcome lullaby, as familiar to her as her own breath. The beach was a scatter of pebbles and large boulders tumbled together. A narrow harbour formed between them, just big enough to fit a couple of rowboats. A dark cave loomed, like a giant's mouth waiting to swallow her whole. Soon, it would be filled with crates of tea and lace and brandy. It meant the difference between a lean, potentially deadly season of hunger and full bellies and bright eyes. Especially over the last couple of years, when the fishing was poor and the price of salt taxed to the hilt by the government. How were they to process and cure even meager hauls of pilchard fish without enough salt? And what would they then eat come winter?

She felt no guilt at all over the smuggling of illegal goods. Not when it fed her siblings and her collection of needy animals. None of them had anywhere else to go. No other recourse. She saved her guilt for other matters.

For Callum.

But not tonight. Tonight, she had to keep a weather eye out. The beach seemed deserted, the pebbles underfoot undisturbed. The strip of sand closer to the water showed no other footsteps but it would be easy enough for someone to walk in the foam, letting the waves wash away every mark. As she was doing right now, shoes in her hand.

She had to clamber around a slippery boulder, pass the spot where the village wainwright had drowned, and then climb up the cliffside to stick her hand in a crevice that housed spiders and mice and the occasional bird's nest.

And a small glass bottle, weathered by time.

She stretched to reach it, contorting her shoulder until muscles strained and complained. King Arthur sat below her, watchful and patient. She finally climbed back down and sat next to him, catching her breath.

It took a moment to decipher the message sent in code: a round white shell, seven pebbles, and a blue bead.

Seven nights past the full moon, care of Captain Davignon who always wore a blue coat.

She had only a week to gather the men and boats. While attending a fancy house party alongside a revenue man. And stealing something valuable from a duke.

Mustn't forget that little detail.

King Arthur pushed his cold wet nose into her palm, sensing her agitation. She smiled down at him. "Not to worry," she said. "It will all sort itself out."

He wagged his tail.

If only she believed her own lies as easily.

She would need landers to arrange the unloading of the cargo. She could help there or with the rowing to and from the ship.

They would need tubsmen to carry any barrels of brandy to the hideouts and a batsman to protect them. She had heard stories of gangs down in Mousehole with up a to hundred men to deal with the unloading, the storage of the contraband in cellars and churches, the selling of it. Little Crumpet had Cat and roughly a dozen men on the shore, a dozen women in the village who were encouraged to watch the wall.

But she would make it work.

She took King Arthur through the edge of the village on their way home, past the Laughing Mermaid pub. The painted sign creaked in the wind, the artwork slightly disconcerting. She wasn't sure mermaids were meant to have that many teeth.

The door was closed but a new notice had been posted to the warped wood. *A Ship has been sighted in this quarter engaging in the unlawful act of Smuggling. Reward of three hundred pounds. This nineteenth day of August, 1803.*

Bollocks.

She'd have to send word to Captain Davignon.

A hundred pounds was an enormous temptation.

As she'd suspected, a lantern burned behind the shuttered window. Were they even now discussing it? The village was loyal, but that sum of money might make the difference between not just empty bellies but also countless new opportunities. Damn the revenue men.

"They've started without you," Granny Goodwin said from the shadows across the street. Cat tried not to jump. She consoled herself with the fact that King Arthur was entirely unbothered. He was used to Granny Goodwin. She sat out on her stoop at all manner of hours, chewing on the end of her pipe and feeding her collection of crows.

Cat envied her the murder of crows. Had done since she was a girl and Granny taught her to feed them bits of apples and cheese.

"Men will do that," Granny continued. Of course, she knew there were plans afoot. She always knew. Not only did she live across the street from the only pub, but she had a downright supernatural ability to eavesdrop. "Best not let them, my girl."

Right.

She was the only one with access to a captain from Guernsey willing to sail to the north of Cornwall. Everyone knew the easy beaches to land on and the established gangs were in the south. They had their own smuggler bankers, for god's sake.

Cat had her mother's affair with a captain over three years ago.

It would have to do.

The others would try to run roughshod over her, to convince her to pass on the location of the message drop, the code, everything.

Like hell.

She knocked softly on the door, two short, pause, three short, pause, one short. She waited, hearing the scrape of a chair leg on the floor, footsteps. Then nothing. "Don't be a git," she said through the crack of the door. "I know you're in there."

Behind her, Granny Goodwin cackled.

When the door finally opened an inch, Cat pushed through with her black dog. Fishermen were a superstitious lot and they tended to give her a wider berth when King Arthur walked at her heels. No one needed to know he limped in the cold now and sometimes had nightmares which required soothing belly scratches. Let them think him an ill omen, a warning.

She intended to need one to announce her.

The pub smelled like spilled ale and fish pies. The innkeeper had gone to bed. He preferred to know no secrets so he could spill no secrets. But everyone who needed it, knew where he kept the key to the back door.

"Cat," Ambrose, the innkeeper's brother, greeted her from his usual spot, cap on his head, tankard in his hand. The others sat on benches or leaned against the counter. Cat counted five, with Little Simon lurking in the kitchen, his ear to the door. "Weren't expecting you."

"Don't see why not," she shot back. She liked Ambrose. He was kind and fair. But she wouldn't let him underestimate her any more than the others. "We said three o'clock. I'm even early." Not as early as they were, mind you.

"So you are."

"Have a seat," Juro offered, pulling out a chair. His pale cheeks were ruddy. He smiled at her and resisted the urge to shudder. Juro she did *not* like. He didn't like her either, which suited her fine. He was a terrible judge of character. But he was wily. And everyone thought they needed wily.

She'd show them wily.

She might not have three fishing boats to her name, but she had a captain. And a key still tucked into her stays.

Offering her a seat seemed a polite gesture, but Cat knew he was trying to point out that she was unsuitable for the hard, physical work of smuggling. That a walk might tire her out. That as a woman, they would need to mind their manners. That she might be offended by the smallest thing. That she might fall for the appraising look he sent in her direction, or the way he stroked the back of her chair which bordered on lewd.

She considered gagging. Loudly.

"Juro?" she asked instead.

"Yes, dove."

"What are you doing?" She stared at him, her expression hard. She would call it her "Duke Look." She suddenly understood this new Callum much better. It worked like a charm. It took only moments before Juro shifted from foot to foot.

"Nothing," he muttered. "Being polite."

Walter laughed. Juro made a fist.

"I'm not here for polite," she said.

"Figured you'd be too busy eating cakes at the big house to be here at all," he sneered at her.

"I can eat cake and do my job, Juro," she said crisply. "Unlike some, I can do two things at once."

His ears turned red. Everyone knew she was referring to the

time he'd capsized his boat because he'd been too busy trying to catch the attention of the weaver's daughter. He was still sore over it. And if he continued to try and undermine her, she'd use far worse against him. She'd work with Ambrose because Ambrose was clever and just. And he wielded his cane like a spear. Juro was temperamental and thought he was much cleverer than he was. A lot handsomer too. Frankly, it was exhausting.

"I've had word," she announced, because she'd had enough of games at the big house, as he put it. "From the captain."

"Finally," Ambrose said. "A spot of good news."

"He'll be here in a week."

After a moment of excited chatter, Walter turned to her.

"You should tell us the signal," he suggested. "Just in case."

"In case of what?" she asked.

"In case you get held up dancing with the toffs," Juro agreed.

She smiled sweetly. "Not a chance."

"Why should we follow her?" Juro snapped. "She's not special."

"I don't have to be special, I have to be smart," she said.

"Just because your mother opened her legs for a—"

Cat pointed at Juro. King Arthur's hackles immediately rose, and he bared his teeth in an impressive growl. He snapped his jaw once, and a string of saliva hit the floor. Juro swallowed the rest of his insult, stumbling back a step.

She'd taught him that trick in exchange for bits of fried sausage.

Worth every bite she'd gone without.

"Call off yer devil," Juro barked.

"No," she replied, pleasant as a lady refusing a second cup of tea.

But she knew she could lose them at the snap of a finger. Once the cargo dropped, there was nothing but their respect for her to keep them from taking all of the goods. She knew they needed her—but they needed to know it too. This wasn't something she could do on credit. She didn't have the time or the opportunity to prove herself. Juro would pour poison in their ears every chance he got.

"I've got the captain," she said. "And I've got the duke's signet ring," she said.

And awed silence fell.

A letter bearing the Tremaine seal would open doors and close eyes that might see too much. That kind of influence to clear the way when cargo was finally ready to be moved was invaluable. And without such an obvious advantage, she might never truly convince the village men to join her operation. To follow her. She had two advantages now: connection to a captain who would only deal with her directly and who traveled to and from Guernsey Island where goods were not subject to British tax, and a duke's signet ring.

Of course, she didn't have the ring.

Not yet.

Chapter Eight

S HE DID NOT get caught sneaking back into the house.

At least not the way in which she might have expected.

There was no footman lurking in the hallway, no scandalized matron with her candle.

Only Callum.

And he did not spring at her out of the shadows. He did not even know she was there.

But she was caught, nonetheless.

The door to his library was partially open, lit by a single candle. He sat in his shirtsleeves, cravat loose, head resting against the scrolled back of a padded chair. His profile could have been a painting, the angle of his jaw, his lips. He was unfairly handsome.

And sad.

And that she could not have.

Cursing herself for being ten times a fool, she knocked very softly. He straightened immediately, the invisible mantle of a duke falling around him, right down to his spine. But she'd caught another glimpse of what still lived underneath.

"Miss Sparrow," he said gruffly.

The way he said her name. *Still* said her name. She had to order her knees very strictly not to soften, her thighs not to heat.

"Did you need something?"

"I couldn't sleep, and I saw your candle. I did not mean to

disturb you," she added.

"You didn't. I'm merely waiting for the traffic outside my bedroom door to disperse," he replied drily. "Do come in."

It was monstrously improper.

Of course, she stepped inside.

There were advantages to not being part of the *ton,* to never being on the Marriage Mart. To being a spinster.

The library had dark Tudor beams and crooked floors, but they were covered with lush carpets. The fireplace mantlepiece was flanked by marble knights. "It did seem a bit… lively upstairs. Are house parties always like that?"

He snorted. "Yes. Although I have never feared someone might actually camp out and sleep in the hall outside my chamber before. Lady Siddal is… determined."

"Are they all waiting for you then?" Cat asked curiously.

"A compromising situation is more permanent than these games of my mother."

She made a face. "I should not like to spend my life with someone who had to be tricked into it." Although she imagined the power and wealth due to a duchess was compensation enough for many, especially when options were scarce on the ground. That she could understand perfectly well.

"They are mirrors," he said. Something about a dark quiet room in the middle of the night invited confidences. "They are displeased when I am displeased. They sigh when I sigh, laugh when I laugh. As do their brothers. And their fathers. It's exhausting."

"I promise not to laugh unless you say something very funny."

"Your kindness is noted."

She grinned, she couldn't help it. "If you don't want to be treated like a duke you should probably stop sounding so very duke-like. Do you remember how to laugh, Callu—Your Grace?"

"I know how to do a great many things," he intoned, and she fancied he might be teasing her. Just a little. "I have had tutors since I was in leading strings. I have had lessons in horseback riding, dancing, Latin, medieval art."

"That sounds useful," she snorted. "No wonder it's driving you to drink." She nodded to the glass on the table. The candlelight sparkled through dark amber liquid. She sniffed. "But driving you to drink *brandy*? That I would never have guessed."

"Don't tell Armstrong," he muttered.

"Is he the new revenue man?" She had not met him but she knew he was in the house, a guest who could unravel her whole life.

"It is. And I doubt he'd look kindly on my contraband."

He'd look on a duke's contraband just fine. Cat's, on the other hand, was a different matter altogether.

"People will insist on giving me gifts," he grumbled.

"I did not bring you a single thing," she told him cheerfully. In fact, she meant to take something from him instead.

"Good."

She knew he would not think that for long. She should go to bed right now, before the soft darkness of this library lulled her into a very false sense of security.

"Why are people giving you illegal brandy?" she asked instead. "That seems... out of character."

"So that I might remember them," he sighed. "And since I can afford the taxes on liquor, they want to prove they are resourceful or interesting or some such rot."

And he hated it. That much she could see.

But self-pity was only good for giving you a sour belly, as her mother had often said.

"Poor you," Cat dropped into the chair beside him without an invitation. He still looked sad; it was there in his eyes, in the tired set of his mouth. "I suppose a friend would help you with your troubles."

She snatched up his glass and tossed back a large mouthful. He was so startled that he forgot to look sad, for just that moment. Cat cleared her throat which was currently on fire. And not in a pleasurable way. "That is *terrible* brandy," she accused.

Callum's mouth twitched. "Unfortunately, it is."

"I'm sorry to tell you this, but whoever gave that to you is no friend." She would have wiped her tongue if she could have. Would have informed him that *her* brandy was of much better quality if she could have. Whoever had let it down to make it drinkable had done an abysmally poor job. Brandy was smuggled over-proof and then diluted. It meant far less volume and fewer casks for the ships to haul. But it also meant people drank awful concoctions. The French would be morally insulted. "Don't drink bandy smuggled into London," she couldn't help but warn him.

He lifted an eyebrow.

"Everyone knows London water will make you ill. But there is one thing you *can* do with bad brandy."

"What's that?"

"Snapdragon."

He frowned. "What?"

"You've never played Snapdragon at Christmas?" she gaped at him.

"My mother did not encourage games or frivolity. Ironic, isn't it?"

"Well, that won't do," Cat announced, standing up. She held out her hand. "Come with me."

"I beg your pardon?"

"We're going to play Snapdragon."

"It's past three in the morning."

"And so no one will see us and your reputation will be safe," she assured him. "Don't worry, anyone who is not asleep is probably loitering by your bedroom door, remember?" He let himself be drawn to his feet. She kept forgetting how tall he was, how wide his shoulders.

Don't get distracted. This is a mission of mercy.

She remembered a Callum who smiled, who laughed. And she was starting to strongly suspect that he had not truly done so since they were young.

He followed her down to the kitchen, mostly because she would not let him refuse. She carried the decanter of smuggled brandy. "Why are you fully dressed?" he asked, behind her. "And wearing shoes?"

Oops.

"I always go for a walk when I can't sleep," she explained as she led him down the stairs to the dark kitchen. At least it was the truth. If not the truth tonight.

She pushed him towards a stool and rummaged for a platter and a jar of raisins and then lit a candle. He watched her as if she was the most interesting creature he had every seen. "Have you ever been down to the kitchens?" she asked.

"Of course," he said. "Cook always had biscuits for me."

She felt better knowing that, for some reason.

His eyes never left her as she scattered raisins in the platter and poured the brandy over them. "I am intrigued and faintly terrified."

She faltered. "This is silly. You don't want to play a children's game."

She drew away but he caught her hand. "Show me, Cat." A command, but a soft one. A shiver tickled the back of her neck.

"Very well." She cleared her throat. "The goal is to snatch the raisins from the platter."

"That doesn't seem so difficult."

She tilted the candle, touching the flame to the liquor. Blue fire kindled in the platter.

Callum stared. "This is meant for children?"

"Well, for everyone, really."

"At Christmas."

"Exactly."

"Did you also leap from the cliffs into the sea at Christmas?" he asked wryly. "For a spot of fun? Juggle knives?"

"Don't be silly," she shot back, biting down on her smile. "We only had two knives to our name. I'll go first."

"By all means."

"The trick is to move fast."

"Clearly."

"And stick to the raisins on the edge. Don't get cocky." She snatched one up and popped it in her mouth. It was warm, but not too hot, and sweet.

"And she eats fire," he murmured. For some reason, it made her feel like blushing.

"Something about the burning brandy makes the fire less hot." She leaned on the table. "Though my sister always went too fast and too far in and burned her tongue."

The mention of her sister reminded her of why she was here. She was about to suggest that she go back to her room. He seemed to sense it, pushed up his sleeves. The light flickered over corded muscles, dark hair. "My turn."

"You don't have to. It's silly."

"Are you calling my honor into question, Miss Sparrow?"

"Certainly, Your Grace."

He chuckled. She was sure of it. It was brief, quiet. Startled. But it was a chuckle.

"Be careful," she added, just as he leaned forward.

He paused, shot her a stern scolding look from under his eyebrows. "Are you cheating?"

"I'm merely making sure the duke doesn't set his very impressive eyebrows on fire."

"I'll have you know I survived a twelve-course meal seated between the Prince of England and a lady who could only talk about her father's cows all while being fed foods set in jelly and the organs of animals dressed in roses. The entire dining room was decorated in puce, from the curtains to the chairs to the dress code requested by the hostess. She had heard it was my favorite color."

Cat smiled with her whole face. "You wore puce?"

"I wore emerald."

"Spoilsport. Who told her it was your favorite color?"

"Blackpool, that degenerate." But he said it fondly, the same way he talked about his sister.

"Still." She held up her hands in mock defeat. "Clearly a little fire is nothing to do that."

"Exactly so." He snatched the raisins from the plate before she could say anything else. He chewed them, nodding. "You're quite right. Bad brandy is much better when it's on fire."

She tried for another raisin and was not quite fast enough. She yanked her hand back with a short hiss, shaking her fingers. "You win, Your Grace."

"Let me see," he said immediately.

"It's fine."

His fingers closed around her wrist. "I said let me see."

She rolled her eyes and let him inspect her nonexistent wound. "No blister," he finally said, satisfied. "No wound."

"I told you, it's nothing. I burn myself much worse baking the bre—"

She broke off when he suddenly drew the tip of her finger into his mouth, sucking it to the first knuckle. His tongue soothed the sting.

And it kindled fire everywhere else.

Everywhere. Else.

Sticking your burned finger in your mouth was instinct. This was something else entirely. His blue eyes met hers and stayed there, even as he sucked gently.

She swallowed, definitely feeling it in her knees. Her thighs. A tingle of warmth moving languidly through her core like honey.

He released her, standing with his perfect posture and his powerful voice suggesting discipline and self-control.

His eyes suggested something else. They burned. Because of her.

"Miss Sparrow." He bowed.

She did not curtsy back.

She was very much afraid her knees had stopped working.

Chapter Nine

D ISASTER.

Absolute disaster.

"You can't be ill," Cat blurted out. "You *never* get ill."

Viola lay in her bed, the yellow coverlet pulled up to her chin. Her nose was pink and rapidly on its way to red. "Well, I'm ill now," she said, her voice scratchy. "I blame Bartholomew."

Cat poured her a cup of tea. She had wrangled horehound lozenges from the housekeeper Mrs. Pepper. She opened a window to let in fresh air. "Better?" she asked hopefully.

"No," Viola sighed.

"I can see about some lemons." Their mother always managed to find enough coin for a single lemon when they came down with a lung complaint or soreness of the throat. "Maybe you'll be better by the afternoon."

"I won't be coming downstairs with a chapped nose, Cat." She sounded deeply offended. "Nor am I going to give a dowager duchess the *sniffles*."

"But…"

Dread trickled through her. The first official challenge was today. If Viola went home, there was no reason for Cat to stay on as chaperone. No other earthly reason for Cat to ever be here, invitation notwithstanding.

Hard to steal from the duke if she didn't have access to his personal belongings.

She would lose the cargo. Any hope of income.

Not to mention that she wasn't even sure how to look him in the eye after last night. He might see that the warmth of it was still coursing through her. The slide of his tongue, the unexpected and very un-dukelike caress.

She very, very much wanted to scream.

"Cat?"

Cat blinked, returning to the room. The way Viola said her name suggested it had not been the first time. Cat sat down heavily on the corner of the bed. "I suppose I shall have to take your place."

Viola sat up, eyes wide. "You will?"

She tried a bolstering smile. "Certainly. You'll be better in a day or so and then you will not have lost your place. We will carry on."

Assuming, of course, that Cat did not come dead last in every challenge. With any luck, swimming would be first up. That at least she could do with a reasonable amount of success.

Viola narrowed her eyes suddenly. "What's going on?"

Cat swallowed. "What do you mean?"

"You hate performing for people."

"I don't hate…" Viola was right. She did hate it. And also, none of her skills would translate to this sort of house party.

"Not to mention that we won't know how to do any of the things the dowager expects," Viola pointed out, voicing Cat's thoughts. "My curtsy was a lucky accident."

"You want this," she said, willing her sister to believe her. "The chance to meet the peerage, whatever comes of these ludicrous Duchess Games." *Please let Viola fall in love with someone other than the duke. The vicar. A stablehand. The scullery maid. Anyone.* "So I'll help."

There was a beat of silence before Viola relaxed against the pillows, grinning. "You are the best sister."

The best sister. But possibly the worst person. Her reasons

were not… good. They were not honourable, however loving her motivations might be. She was sacrificing Callum for her family. He was a duke, she reminded herself yet again. He would survive this.

She might not survive what he would surely do to her when it was all over.

Or the thought of what he might have done to her were things very different.

"And you'll be right as rain after a little rest," she added out loud, mostly because her sister was looking at her again.

Viola sneezed. Violently.

THE NEXT TASK took them to the gardens for which Cat was grateful. Sunshine, fresh air, grass under her shoes. Well, crushed seashell pathways and too many roses that tickled the nose, but close enough.

She'd hoped for lawn bowling. Swimming. Leaping the hedges like a horse. Deboning a haddock.

Not…watercolors.

Cat was not particularly artistically inclined. She'd drawn as a child, like all children, with bits of charcoal from the fire or with a stick in the sand on the beach. Not on thick paper that cost more than her dress. With fancy pencils and soft paintbrushes made of sable and paint that had traveled all the way from London.

The dowager duchess spent a good half an hour terrorizing the ladies by wandering between them like a general running a military drill. She peered down her nose at shading and brushstrokes and composition. She blinked at Cat's decidedly lopsided hedge complete with roses that looked painfully squashed. And slightly bloody, truth be told. She sniffed. Honestly, Cat couldn't blame her.

Summer met her gaze and rolled her eyes. Unsurprisingly, Summer's rendering of a Greek statue was perfect. More than that, she had true talent. Even Cat could tell. Her technique was no doubt the result of years of lessons with painting masters, but her choices were her own. The shading was deeper where it might have been light, light where it might have been dark. She used unexpected colors to make the marble gleam, the leaves glow.

Cat made a lovely mud color. Several times. Despite never using brown of any kind. Her trees looked unwell.

Lady Imogen's trees looked like the saint of painting had taken her by the hand.

Cat was fairly certain Viola had her nose pressed to the window behind them and was laughing at her. Cat wiped her paintbrush and chose a bright, cheerful red. May as well have fun with it.

Oh dear, her berries looked even more like blood.

She would call it *A Garden Massacre*.

Lady Imogen glanced at them and then offered a pained smile. Cat just grinned. Lady Imogen squeaked. Cat frowned at her easel. That reaction was a bit much. And then Lady Imogen curtsied low, far too low for someone covered in paint. Except Lady Imogen wasn't covered in paint. Neither was Lady Summer or Lady Siddal or anyone else. Only Cat. Because, of course.

And they were curtsying because Callum had decided to join them.

Or else he'd been hiding in the hedges and had not realized he would stumble right into the lion's den. Cat's money was on the latter.

If she had any money, that was.

"Your Grace," Lady Ruby wore a yellow dress today and it glowed against the backdrop of green leaves and white roses. Cat would not be surprised if she'd bribed someone on the household staff first thing in the morning in order to know where they would be situating so as to better match her surroundings. She was stunning. Her curtsy was stunning, her painting was stunning.

So why was Callum walking towards Cat? Glowering, as usual. If only his glower weren't quite so... stirring. She was sure it said something unsavory about her character. That she liked being the object of all of that dark focus.

But she was tucked into the furthest spot from his mother and from the other guests taking tea and offering suggestions and critiques, for a reason. Discretion being a part of valor, she much preferred not to be noticed at such an event. Especially as Viola ought to be here instead.

Callum stopped. Dozens of pairs of calculating eyes bored into her back. Because she wanted to scrunch up her shoulders, she squared them instead.

"That is an…interesting interpretation," Callum said. She couldn't read his tone. It was very, very bland. If he'd been anyone else she might have thought he was teasing. There was no sign of the man who had sucked her finger into his mouth as if she was a delicacy.

"That's one way to put it." She wasn't too bothered about her abysmal painting. And she did not need to be told that she did not belong, that much was obvious. They would delight in telling her though. Callum's mother had turned this into a glittering, courteous battlefield. There would be blood. And not just on her canvas.

She might have returned to her paints with the kind of stubbornness that did not always do her any favors except for the rustle in the juniper bush. And a tiny sound.

She knew that sound.

She darted around her easel; Callum and the realization that she hadn't curtsied to him like she ought to, forgotten. Well, she *might* have forgotten him if he hadn't insisted on pacing behind her like a mildly threatening storm cloud. She crouched in the grass, her voice a gentle murmur. "Come along, you little troublemakers."

A rustle. A tiny mew.

"It's no use," she said, pushing aside the branches. "I know you're there."

"Have you found another turtle?" Callum asked.

"Afraid not," she said, emerging from the leaves with handfuls of kittens. "I found these instead."

"Kittens," he said, nonplussed. She may as well have told him she had found three clowns. "In the junipers."

They were gray and white, squirming tiny drunken gentlemen, like all kittens. "They are far too young," she said, as a small very sharp fang sank into her arm. "Ouch. Don't be rude."

There was a chorus of meowing, more squirming. Cat stood up, grinning.

"You look well pleased," Callum remarked.

"I don't think they would have survived for long out here if we hadn't found them. Who knows what's happened to their mother?" Her smile faltered at the thought. Callum stepped closer. "But now they'll survive, at least."

"I had no idea this estate had turned into a zoological garden," he said drily, still watching her carefully. As if she might fall and he might need to catch her.

"Wouldn't that be lovely?" She was momentarily distracted at the thought. What a fine use for so much land. She shook her head, returning to the moment when one of the kittens swiped at the other.

"*What* is that noise they are making?" Callum asked.

"We call that screaming."

"It's…most unpleasant."

"Not everyone has the manners of a duke."

"Pity."

"They are hungry, poor devils. This one is far too tiny to be alone. And these two do not care for each other at all." She shoved a hissing animal at Callum. He took it out of instinct and the kitten immediately attacked his cravat. If kittens could cackle gleefully, this one would have done so.

"If you give me fleas, I'll make you into stew," Callum said. Cat glanced up, remembering that one did not shove dirty angry kittens at dukes. Callum's hand was gentle under the kitten and there was a smile lurking under his disapproving tone.

"Well, come along," Cat said briskly, turning on her heel. She marched away without waiting to see if he would join her. The smaller of the kittens tucked his head awkwardly into the neckline of her dress and promptly went limp with sleep. The other one stared at her suspiciously, still mewling.

"Dare I ask where you are taking me?" Callum asked. "In my own home?"

"To the kitchens," she tossed over her shoulder. She paused to flutter her eyelashes at him. "Unless you'd prefer I bring them to your chambers? We could set up a basket on your bed. They will sing you to sleep and bite your toes."

He narrowed his eyes at her. "No, thank you."

She smothered a laugh. "Very well, the kitchens it is."

"I was joking about the stew, you know."

"They need a bath, a meal, and a warm basket," Cat explained. "Your cook and your housekeeper will be able to assist me."

Except that the kitten had wrapped himself entirely around his arm and would not be moved. By the time they reached the kitchens, Cat was covered in little scratches. Callum frowned at her chest. She blinked. "What?" When she followed his gaze she added. "Oh, that's fine. Hardly the first time."

"You'll wash those."

"Obviously."

"And apply a vinegar rinse."

She wrinkled her nose. "I don't usually bother, to be honest."

"Miss Sparrow, I may not know much about wrangling turtles but even I know that cat scratches can fester." He sounded furious with her, but she thought it might actually be concern. She wasn't sure what to do with either.

They set the kittens, still whimpering for food, inside a harvesting basket left by the rosemary bush. Cat went down into the kitchens and wrangled a basin, hot water, and soap, as well as goat milk and egg yolk with a bit of gelatin for the kittens. She washed her hands and arms first, and even wiped at her decolletage—mostly because Callum glowered at her.

By the time the kittens had been washed and were starting to feed, they had gathered an audience of Cook, three maids, two footmen and two gardeners. Competing advice was offered, sometimes rather forcefully. The kittens fell asleep in a pile in their basket, rounded bellies quivering with snores. She thought the Cook might snatch them into her apron. "Poor wee things," she kept saying. She wouldn't look at the duke, but she raised her voice. "We have a fierce mouse problem belowstairs. Can't keep them from the larder. Hard to make blackberry tarts that way."

By the way Callum sighed, Cat deduced that blackberry tarts were his favorite, and everyone knew it. "Set one of the scullery maids or the gardener's boys in charge of the kittens until they're old enough to mouse."

Cat opened her mouth.

"And consult Miss Sparrow as to their proper care."

Cat beamed at him, before remembering she shouldn't beam at a duke. At Callum. "Thank you."

He just grunted and walked away.

Chapter Ten

DINNER THAT NIGHT was held in the formal dining where a forest of candles burned clean, warming the air with the smell of honey. This house had never seen tallow. The light gleamed off the gilded frames of seascape paintings and portraits of Tremaine ancestors with their favorite cows. It glittered off the gold candelabras, the gold stitching of the tablecloth, the gold ribbons wound around centrepieces of hothouse flowers she'd never seen before and no less than three pineapples. It struck crystal drops from the chandeliers, diamond necklaces, silver cravat pins. It was dazzling.

And it threatened to give Cat a headache.

She knew her place and it was not in this room at this dinner. It was certainly not near the head of the table, sitting next to a duke. Covered in cat scratches.

Despite what the duke's sister might have to say about it.

"Of course you'll sit right here," Summer said, personally showing her to the chair with its seat embroidered with oak leaves and the arms carved with acorns. "I'm sorry to hear your sister is not feeling well but as she won the challenge, you must take her place," Summer announced cheerfully and quite loudly. She looked down at the seated guests, some of whom exchanged glances Cat chose not to decipher. The only people present who would dare contradict her were her mother and her brother.

The dowager duchess frowned, likely on principle. It was bad enough that Viola had charmed her, but her spinster sister might be too much to be borne. Before she could speak however, Callum drew Cat's chair back. "Allow me, Miss Sparrow."

A duke personally seating said spinster. Even the footman hovering behind them, whose job had just been usurped, was not sure what to do. A curious, gossipy silence thrummed.

Cat sat down, practically jumping into the chair, mostly because it afforded her less of the intense attention than would have any kind of refusal or demurral. "Thank you," she murmured.

Callum nodded to the butler, who nodded to the footmen, who in turn leapt into action. A blur of movement surrounded them as the soup course was served. Ladies removed their gloves and placed them on their laps. Cat followed suit, never having worn gloves to dinner before. At least not all practicality had been tossed out of the window. Although even she knew the pineapples on gold trays were a display of wealth and privilege, not meant to be eaten, only admired. And often rented for parties such as this one before traveling on to other balls and suppers and betrothal announcements.

And as a fisherman's daughter, Cat had never had previous cause to be introduced to the gentleman seated beside her. She knew he was the Earl of Blackpool, but she did not know if she was supposed to pretend *not* to know. Did they still need to be introduced by another party? What were the rules? She was confident she could eat her soup without slurping and comment on the weather with the best of them, but that was about it. She didn't want to embarrass her sister.

She didn't want to embarrass herself in front of Callum.

Which was absurd. Ridiculous. Neither here not there.

Also, uncomfortably true.

"Miss Sparrow, forgive my forwardness but I cannot abide a silent meal," the earl said, all ease and smiles as the soup bowls were removed. "Allow me to introduce myself to you." He tilted his head closer, whispering. "If you promise not to tattle on me to the duchess for my scandalous manners."

Cat smiled. "I promise."

"Excellent. Lord Blackpool at your service."

The earl clearly lived up to his reputation for charm. There was a kindness under the practiced smirk of a rake, for him to put her at her ease. Many would not have bothered. In fact, Cat was suddenly quite sure that was the reason he was sitting next to her, precedence be damned. The dowager duchess would certainly have considered the comfort of the earl, but not necessarily that of a girl beneath her notice who would be forgotten by morning. Summer was different.

"Your sister has a curtsy to make angels weep. As the eldest, I assume you taught her?"

Cat chuckled. "Definitely not. Her prowess is entirely self-won. And I'm afraid she inherited all of the grace in the family," she added fondly.

"Miss Sparrow," Lord Blackpool practically purred. She felt it despite herself. "I refuse to believe that."

He was slightly too close. Slightly too forward.

"You are entirely too modest," he added. He fairly smoldered at her. He was very good at it. But it only made her want to pat his hand fondly, like a cousin might.

"Blackpool," Callum said sharply. Something shivered in his hard tone, like a shark moving under dark still waters. Cat did not quite understand it.

Lord Blackpool, clearly, did. He paused, then he sat back abruptly, grinning. It was not the reaction Cat expected. Callum, however, clearly had every confidence that one word spoken would have an effect. He went back to his meal.

"Shall I apologize, Miss Sparrow?"

"Not at all."

Lord Blackpool sent Cat one last warm, conspiratorial smile before turning to the companion on his left.

"It's that glad I am, you've come home, Your Grace," Mr. Armstrong said. She had managed to find out who he was by asking one of the maids. He was seated slightly too far away from the duke to be engaging in polite conversation. But he was clearly on fire with the need.

A revenue man to the core.

He was new to the area and that never boded well. He was middle-aged, handsome, and clearly from another county altogether. There wasn't a hint of the Cornishman about him. He would want to prove himself. He must be the new supervisor the other agents had been waiting on.

"It's a defiant village," he added with distaste. "We need the steadying influence of a duke."

"Is that so?" Callum asked mildly. He slid a glance at Cat out of the corner of his eye.

She was suddenly very interested in her glass of wine.

"Full of smugglers and wreckers, I don't mind telling you."

"Is this true?" Lady Imogen asked on a gasp, staring at Cat. Mr. Armstrong followed her gaze.

"Are you the girl from the village then?"

The girl. He was barely ten years older than her. She ground her back teeth. "I am, sir." She lowered her eyes. She knew it made her appear meek but really she just needed to hide her scowl. She could not let him see her react, could not be memorable.

"I hope you're grateful for this opportunity to be among your betters. You might take what you learn back to your village."

She fully intended to.

But not the way he assumed.

Callum's head snapped up. "I beg your pardon?"

"But I'm sure you're good and proper. And you'd send word if you saw something suspicious."

"Of course, sir." Bollocks to that.

"Send word to me directly, at Mr. Popewell's."

Bloody burning bollocks.

Mr. Popewell was the nosiest, most sanctimonious man in the village.

"Mr. Armstrong, I applaud your dedication to the law," Callum said.

Of course, he would.

"And I am also quite certain you did not mean to suggest one of my guests might have unsavory associations? And a woman, at that."

Mr. Armstrong blanched. "Of course not, Your Grace. The ladies are far too dainty for that sort of thing."

Cat stifled a snicker. She'd never been called dainty in her entire life.

And she knew perfectly well that Callum was not defending her but defending the honor of his title and his house and whatever tiresome posturing that was required by a duke. She still liked it though. Too much. While Mr. Armstrong went pale, she might blush inappropriately at any moment.

"But what's a wrecker?" one of the ladies asked.

Mr. Armstrong explained with a grim gleefulness generally reserved for ghost stories and children. His sideburns practically quivered with indignation. "Wreckers are the scourge of good God-fearing sailors, and a particular stain on Cornwall."

Cat doubted very much that wreckers were not found along every coast of England.

She did not say so, of course. However much she longed to.

"The tin miners and the fishermen of this county put out false lights to draw ships onto the rocks and dash them to pieces."

As expected, a shocked gasp from the London visitors.

Cat clenched her teeth together harder. Shipwrecks did happen, as they happened everywhere. And claims were made immediately to salvage the debris, she wouldn't deny it. When cargo barrels floated into reach, or trunks of clothes, all hands tried for their piece. But the idea that the villagers of Little Crumpet crept along the shoreline with lanterns to murder dozens of sailors for their possible goods was gossip, pure and simple.

"But why?" Lady Imogen breathed.

"So that the Cornishmen might row out and steal every bit of cargo, every lamp and floorboard for themselves. Just imagine them plucking boots and brandy bottles from between the bobbing bodies, drowned and broken from the crash. It's an unlawful people, either stinking of fish or covered in soot from the mines. No regard for the proper order of things."

"How awful," Lady Imogen said. "I had no idea."

Cat might not know the rules of proper etiquette at a duke's table but punching a fellow guest was probably frowned upon.

"Are we quite safe here, do you think?" Summer, a Cornish-woman if not a villager, asked. Mr. Armstrong did not notice the sarcasm laced through her words.

"Not to fear, the King's own revenue men are here." He straightened, like a hero in a fairy tale. "And we mean to catch every one of them. Smugglers, wreckers, criminals all. We have plans, you see."

This dinner might be awkward and interminable—just like the entire week promised to be—but she might yet learn something of value. If she could keep herself wholly uninteresting to Mr. Armstrong, she might discover a useful detail or two. It was risky, of course. Being in the close company of custom agents always was.

"A problem to be sure," Callum said sternly. "Let us discuss it privately, Armstrong."

"It would be my honor, Your Grace."

Trust a duke to be so amenable to a revenue man. Cat kept her eyes on her plate lest her expression give her away. A spinster out of her depths was a much more useful shield than the tirade she desperately wished to unleash. A defense of her fellow Cornishmen, a reminder that the tax on salt made it impossible to store food, to work leather or glass. To live. A tax on brandy might irritate the *ton,* but they could drown their tears in champagne.

And the finest French brandy she intended to smuggle.

Not like that swill Callum drank.

Luckily, the footmen returned with a procession of platters before her shield could crack. There was baked trout, oysters in their shell, lobster bisque, peas with butter and thyme, slices of lamb with mint sauce, a pie filled with duck, potatoes and carrots, spears of asparagus and partridges roasted in honey and sage. Wine glasses were refilled, mouths were discreetly blotted with napkins.

Cat had never seen so much food. And there were still two more courses left. She was accustomed to bread and potatoes and endless pilchard fish so salty it was known to give an enthusiastic eater mouth ulcers. With illegal salt, naturally. A family such as the Winters had likely never had pilchard in their entire lives, though it was a staple of livelihood in the villages, both for fishermen to sell and to see one through the winter. Apparently, it was considered a delicacy in Rome.

It did *not* smell nice.

At least not while being processed before it reached fine Roman mansions. Or estates such as Penhallow.

Poor Viola, eating toast and beef tea in her room. At least it wasn't pilchard. Still, Cat gave a half-serious thought as to how she could smuggle lamb slices upstairs.

"How does your sister fare? Does she require a doctor?" Callum asked her as she eyed the peas and the likelihood of filling her gloves without anyone noticing. Best not. "I would be happy to send for one."

Cat shook her head. "Thank you, she is well enough. Just a bit of the sniffles." She realized as soon as she said it that she was probably not supposed to discuss sniffles and people's noses over partridges. She dropped her gaze to a smear of mint sauce on her plate.

No planting facers, no talk of bodies, no peevish defense of her county.

Proper etiquette was a pain the arse.

"I'm glad to hear it," Callum said. "I am certain she is a better patient than my sister."

"I am the soul of grace and dignity," Summer protested.

"Until your nose swells up," he snorted. He was easier with his sister, those harsh edges softened.

Apparently, dukes and their sisters could talk about noses.

"I am a duke's sister," she said with mock offense. "I assure you my nose does not *swell*."

"Only your head," Lord Blackpool muttered.

Summer's eyes narrowed instantly. "What was that?"

"Nothing," he drawled. "Nothing at all."

Chapter Eleven

AFTER A COURSE of enough cheese to empty the estate dairy had been shared between the guests, the dowager duchess rose. The ladies followed her lead, retiring to the drawing room as the gentlemen remained at the table with glasses of port. Mr. Armstrong made a joke about smuggled brandy.

Cat blinked at him as if she didn't understand what he was saying. She did not look at Callum.

It was not easy.

The ladies drank tea brought to them by yet more footmen in curled white wigs, only worn in the most traditional of households. The tea did not have even the faintest whiff of oilskin bags used to smuggle them across the Channel. Cat had to admit it was delicious, more so than the smuggled kind.

She had seated herself alone, perched on the end of a settee at the edge of the main conversation, as far from the dowager duchess as was possible without hanging out of the window. She did not want to draw attention to herself. She was already outside of her element, invited to be part of the décor, not in the spotlight. Her seat at dinner, and her adventure with Callum in the pond was not supporting the natural order of things as demanded by the dowager duchess. Cat could see it in the purse of her lips, followed by the deliberate refusal to further acknowledge a girl from the village.

But unfortunately, Cat needed to stay exactly where she was. She would hide behind the draperies if it meant not being sent home yet.

Lady Ruby joined her, accepting a teacup painted with yellow roses from a footman with three other footmen jostling to beat him to it. Cat didn't blame them. Lady Ruby was that beautiful. She might have been made of porcelain, except for the sharpness in her eyes. "Is your sister truly ill? Because she is the only worthy opponent, and I shall be put out if she has to leave."

Cat smiled. "I assure you she feels the same."

Lady Ruby sent her a sidelong glance. "Is this part of some curious strategy?"

"She is unwell, though it's not serious."

Lady Ruby nodded decisively. "I'll send my maid with a honey tea. It never fails to sort me out."

"That's very kind of you."

"I assure you, I am rarely accused of kindness." Her mouth was a perfect rosebud. She didn't smile but Cat had the impression that she hardly smiled. Some people didn't. She didn't take it personally.

"Kindness takes many forms."

Lady Ruby paused. Her inscrutable expression shifted, but only by a whisper. "They will eat you alive."

Cat laughed. "I'm a village girl, Lady Ruby. They would find me salty and unpalatable."

"Good." Her mouth quirked. "May they choke on you."

CHOKING, UNFORTUNATELY, WAS next on the schedule.

The dowager duchess waited for the gentlemen to join them before declaring a musicale performance would round out the evening. She looked straight at Cat when she spoke. Cat had garnered too much attention already. The balance must be righted. She must be put back in her place, her unsuitability for these games underscored.

Cat knew it. The dowager knew it. Everyone knew it.

And to make a fuss now would only make things so much worse.

Chairs were set out in rows facing a polished pianoforte. It would come as no surprise to anyone that Cat had never learned to play a pianoforte. Where would she have had the chance? And even if they could have afforded such an instrument—which they absolutely could not—where would they have put it? The wolfhounds took up all of the available space. She would have to sleep on the roof.

Three other ladies went first, no doubt to put Cat's humiliation in proper perspective. Lady Imogen's voice was soft and delicate and her talent at the keys clearly the result of hundreds of hours of practice. Lady Ruby shone, sitting straight as a sword on the padded bench, her fingers flying with elegant perfection. Lady Siddal was sophistication itself.

The guests smiled, some swaying in tune, some smirking when a note went awry under another lady's fingertips. Cat only heard perfection, but she could tell by the exchanged glances when a note was skipped or changed. They were used to this sort of entertainment, and they knew these songs as well as they knew the lullabies of their childhood. It was a performance in order to showcase one's talents, one's beauty. Romantic songs, sad songs, all chosen with the care of a general entering a battle.

Cat did not know Mozart or Bach.

Cat knew songs about fish.

Songs about tempests and men drowned and naughty escapades. About taking down the revenue men and running them out of town. They were not suitable for a drawing room, nor a dowager duchess.

Ah well. If her father and her brother could face twenty-foot swells and leaky boats and torn nets, she could face this.

If only Callum were anywhere else on earth but sitting in the front row, the candlelight glinting off his dark hair, his expression inscrutable. The ladies glanced at him, glanced away, desperate for even the barest hint of attention. Lord Blackpool lounged beside him like a cat in the pigeon house. He gathered all of the sultry glances, the blushes. They understood him. He put them at their ease.

Callum did not.

Would not.

Lady Siddal curtsied to the applause that was her due and then found her seat. She knew she had done well, golden hair glowing as she sang. The dowager nodded to her and then turned her head, cold gaze spearing Cat on the spot. "Miss Sparrow, do take your turn."

Cat stood slowly, aware of her simple dress, the key inside her bodice, and the weight of Callum's gaze though she refused to look at him. She smiled politely. "I am afraid I cannot play the pianoforte, my lady." Sea shanties were meant to be sung on the decks of rolling ships while hauling fish or pulling ropes.

The dowager sniffed. Someone chuckled. "Still, you will take your turn. Surely you can sing."

"Like an angel, I'm sure," Callum said quietly. There was a smattering of laughter.

Cat stripped off her gloves, her plump arms scratched, her nails short. She moved to the sideboard before taking her place on the padded bench by the intimidating pianoforte. If she was going to make a fool of herself, she may as well do a thorough and spectacular job of it.

The Sparrows did not falter.

They did not play the pianoforte. But they did play the spoons, like any family from the village. Musical instruments that could be made from household items or driftwood were a particular favorite. They might not dance choreographed steps, but they danced on the beach, and they sang to make the work go faster.

She was absolutely sure no one had ever sung a sea shanty while playing gold spoons.

She grinned because there was nothing left but to commit to the madness of the moment.

She fit the spoons back-to-back, her forefinger secure between the handles. She struck them down against her knee and then back up against the palm of her other hand. They made a clear beat, not as deep as the wooden spoons she used at home, but pretty, nonetheless. She stifled a wince at the thought of the gold denting.

Nothing for it now.

She lifted her voice, and it was passable, plain, perfectly ordinary, but strong.

"I thought I heard the Old Man say; "Leave her, Johnny, leave her. Tomorrow ye will get your pay."

It was strange to sing it alone, without a round of answering voices for the chorus. Ambrose had a terrible singing voice and everyone loved to hear him belt every word from his heart.

"And it's time for us to leave her; Leave her, Johnny, leave her; Oh, leave her, Johnny, leave her."

The guests shifted in their seats, looking at each other. The dowager pursed her lips. She had very possibly never heard a work song in her entire life. Callum's foot tapped discretely and perfectly on beat. No one else noticed.

She noticed.

"For the voyage is long and the winds don't blow."

No one stood up to demand she leave, which she considered a personal triumph.

Better yet, another voice joined her for the next line: *"And it's time for us to leave her."*

She might have imagined it as the next line was reserved for the lead voice and she was alone again. *"Oh, the wind was foul and the sea ran high."*

But sure as the tide, a deep voice joined her again for the next: *"Leave her, Johnny, leave her."*

Cold, reserved Callum was singing along with her, clearly familiar with the old sea shanty. He stood and the scornful glances tossed her way withered into surprise. They bloomed into something far less pleasant when they realized the duke was not just singing along, but he had risen to stand beside her like any courting beau.

She absolutely would not read anything into it.

Oh, but a soft and secret part of her was desperate to hold on to the moment. The flush of pleasure, the surprise of being seen and admired, if only for the sake of courtesy.

Yes, courtesy. Surely that was it.

Never mind that the duke was hardly known for this kind of courtesy. He was better known for taciturn, clipped responses to the softest of questions. And this new "courtesy" would absolutely backfire on her the moment she was alone with any of the ladies. Or their fathers, hoping to trade their daughters for access to power.

For now, it was enough to feel the warmth of him at her side, to hear the way their voices wove together, like roses climbing a trellis. *"And it's time for us to leave her; Leave her, Johnny, leave her; Oh, leave her, Johnny, leave her; For the voyage is long and the winds don't blow; And it's time for us to leave her."*

As the last of the song died away and the spoons went still in her hand there was a charged, uncertain silence. Callum was so close she could have leaned against him. She didn't, of course. But she *wanted* to.

He returned to his seat without a single glance in her direction.

"Do play something a little more genteel, Lady Malborough," the dowager suggested coolly.

One thing was certain.

Cat would not be sitting next to Callum at dinner tomorrow.

Chapter Twelve

CAT COULD NOT sleep.

That was nothing new. She hadn't had a full night's sleep since before her father was lost at sea. When her mother died a few years later, sleep had all but fled. It was up to her to take care of her family. Sleep was too busy counting how much flour cost or wondering if the oncoming storm would cross Matthew's path when he was out on the boat. Or trying to figure out where the revenue men were lurking and how to avoid them. Last year, it had not been much of a problem. She had figured out their routes and their schedules in less than two weeks. But this year, they seemed to be everywhere. And so, sleep had no use for her. Even here in the softest bed this side of an actual cloud.

It was too quiet. She couldn't hear dogs snuffling, cats chasing each other through the yard or Mrs. Mckinnon who liked to sing naked in her front yard when the moon was full. She claimed it was good luck (no one who heard her could say the same). She couldn't even hear the sea from up here on the cliff.

At home she would have started the bread or gone for a wander with Percival, who was always up for a walk as long as he could trot by her side. Someone had dropped a giant wolfhound and her two puppies on their doorstep just a few months ago. It wasn't even anyone from Little Crumpet—word had traveled as far as Tintagel that the Sparrow cottage would not turn away an animal.

Wolfhounds were not cheap to feed. They ate more than Matthew, and that was saying something.

Worry continued to nibble at her, and she knew from long experience that lying in the dark would only make it worse. She sighed and kicked free of the coverlet. A short walk would sort her out.

She tucked the key into her palm and moved through the dark house, not bothering with a candle. She took the back stairs all the way down to the kitchens. She may as well check on the kittens while she was awake. She found them tumbling over each other in the lap of Cook who fed them from a small bladder. She wore a shawl which offered endless entertainment to them, batting the fringes and the knots.

"Up late, ye are," she said. "Can I fetch you some tea?" Cat shook her head and Cook paused. "Beg your pardon," she added, with a crisp London accent, all trace of Cornwall wiped from her speech. She sat up straighter. "How about some bread and cheese?"

"No, thank you." Cat tilted her head. "You don't have to do that on my account."

Cook sighed. "The duchess prefers it. Cornish accents are not fine enough."

"I'm hardly the duchess," Cat pointed out wryly. She leaned forward to scratch a soft ear, a milk-full belly. "I was coming to feed them but I see you have it all in hand."

"Aye, Miss."

"Oh, please call me Cat. I'm sorry, I didn't mean to make more work for you. I can take them upstairs if you like. So you can get some sleep."

Cook tightened her hold on the wriggling mass of fur and teeth and tiny meows. Cat may as well have threatened to use them for slippers. "These wee devils are mine now."

Cat smiled. "What have you named them?"

"Salt, Pepper, and Egg." She nuzzled the largest kitten. "This one's Egg."

"Perfect. He is rather round. I suppose I should leave you to it then." It was odd to be awake with nothing that needed her immediate attention. No mending to be done, no knitting, no baking.

Nothing but the key tucked into her palm. Taunting her. Goading her.

Stealing a gentleman's signet ring was beyond the pale. Stealing one from the duke? Well, she could hang in the market square for it. Who would feed her family then? But who would feed them now? Anyway, she had no intention of defrauding him.

A small ruse. Nothing that would hurt him. But it would make all of the difference to her. It had to be enough to save her family. Her animals. The village.

She softened her steps, glad that she hadn't bothered with slippers. The house was quiet around her, but she couldn't afford to take any chances. The key opened the duke's bedroom but she hoped she would not have to venture there. Surely, he kept his ring in the library with his important things. Whatever those were. Ledgers, letters. *Ducal* things. Most gentlemen wore them daily as a sign of their title and prestige. They protected them from thieves.

Like her.

Except for Callum, apparently, who left his in the unlocked library, on his desk.

No key required.

Foolish, foolish man.

Or a confident one. Only an idiot would steal from the Duke of Tremaine.

Or a village girl.

The ring was simple heavy gold, the family coat of arms engraved on a blue stone cabochon: a simplified anchor and three acorns. She picked it up gently, as if he would somehow sit up in bed several stories above her head when she touched it. As if he'd know she was here. As if she was betraying the moment they had shared just last night, on this very spot.

A floorboard creaked in the hall. Panicked, Cat tossed about for a place to hide the ring. Her nightdress had no pockets. She wasn't even wearing any shoes.

If she put the ring back down on the desk, she might never get close enough again to steal it.

Another footstep.

Her heartbeat was so loud in her ears that it nearly drowned it out. She couldn't escape the study now, couldn't pretend she wasn't standing right here, utterly unbidden. So pulled the window open and tossed the ring into the garden. With any luck, she could retrieve it in a few hours. She tried to relax the line of her spine, the angle of her shoulders. *Carry no guilt, be accused of no guilt.* Ambrose repeated it every time she gathered the smugglers for a run.

All two runs.

Last year.

Each run this year had been aborted at the last minute, damn the revenue men.

"Miss Sparrow."

She froze.

Of course, it was Callum who found her. His rough voice filled with disapproval, moving over every inch of her skin. She curled her bare toes under her nightdress. "Cal—Your Grace."

Something flickered in his face, but it was too quick, and the corridor was too dark for her to read it properly. "What are you doing in here?" he asked.

She smiled carelessly, as if this was all perfectly normal. "I couldn't sleep and I saw an owl pass by the window. I followed it here."

"In my library."

She pointed to the dark gardens, the sky just beginning to glow like a pearl. "Out there, of course. Though, I am sorry. I'm afraid I get rather single-minded when it comes to creatures of all kinds."

Lead with the truth and the lie will disappear like mist in the sunshine. Another of Ambrose's sayings.

She had put herself in all manner of compromising situations in pursuit of an animal who needed help. This was the most normal part of her day, usually. Callum crossed the gleaming floor to stand by her side. She prayed he wouldn't look down. She pointed hastily up and the side, where the house jutted out. "There," she said. "I lost the owl but I found a hawk's nest on the edge of the roof just there."

"I see."

What would it be like if she were truly one of these ladies? At ease with decorum, with shining hair and silk nightdresses. She would be in no less of a social pickle, but she might be able to enjoy the danger of it. She might flirt, lean in closer. Callum might even notice.

But she wasn't a Lady Sparrow.

She was just Cat.

Did he think she was here hoping for another repeat of last night? Mortifying. Tempting.

She felt every freckle on her nose, the swing of her nightdress against her wide hips, the dog hair no doubt on her hem. The scratches on her arms. The key in her hand. The falsehoods shining from her pores like light.

She eased back, eager to get him away from the window, away from his desk. "I should go, I suppose. Back to bed."

His eyes flared. She swallowed, waiting for an interrogation. Instead, he merely agreed. "That would be best."

She tried not to run pell-mell out of there as if her hair was on fire. Calm. Collected. Innocent. When he followed her, she nearly tripped in her relief.

She would take smuggling over housebreaking and burglary any day. Her stomach pitched to and fro like a leaky boat in a storm.

An oil lamp had been left burning at the top of the stairs, throwing enough light to pick her way under a line of family portraits, eyeing her with disapproval. Several old men with wigs, women with diamonds as big as eggs. She turned down the hall, eager to get back to her room where she could panic in peace. She'd have to count the windows to know which was his library from the outside, and then come up with a plausible reason for lurking in the bushes.

"Miss Sparrow, the guest wing is the other way."

She stumbled to a stop. Damn it. So much for not acting flustered.

He looked down his ducal nose at her. He stood strong and steady, as though he was on a ship, not in a hall filled with art and gold and candlelight. Not at all adrift, the way she was. "Miss Sparrow, you do not belong here."

She knew that.

Didn't he think she already knew that?

And why did a simple truth simply spoken feel like cold water poured down the back of her?

Clearly last night was an aberration. And worse, he now thought that she was like the others, sniffing around his door to gain from the title. She wished she could be offended, wished it wasn't true.

She forced a smile even though it felt like a grimace. She added a curtsy, salt to her wounds. "Of course, Your Grace."

THEY WOULD EAT her alive.

She absolutely did not belong here. Wandering around alone at night chasing owls and then turning down the family wing corridor in her nightdress. Too near his bedchamber. His bed. She'd be ruined before breakfast. They'd scorn her and disdain her and send her home with her reputation in tatters.

Like hell.

Not while this was his house.

Not only was it monstrously hypocritical for anyone here to pretend that they did not spend their nights in bedrooms other than their own, but Cat was under his protection. Always. She didn't know it. No one else knew it either. But they'd find out soon enough if he was pushed even an inch.

Never mind the urge to shield her, the urge to stalk her backwards through the open door and into his chambers was deep and dark. Primal. He could see her there with the candlelight shining through the thin material of her nightdress, outlining her soft thighs, her generous hips. He felt a little mad at the thought.

Especially as it was immediately followed with Cat in his bed, nightdress on the floor where it belonged and she dressed in his body alone, pressing down over her—where *he* belonged. He needed to know the taste of her. The sweetness of each nipple, the honey of her quim.

He groaned, rubbing a hand over his face in frustration. He was not going to survive these damn Duchess games.

Because he already had a duchess.

And she would never know it.

Chapter Thirteen

Y OU DON'T BELONG *here.*

Try as she might, Cat could not stop it from reverberating inside her skull. It had whispered to her throughout the long dawn, tainting her sleep until she woke with a mild headache and a not-so-mild case of annoyance. At herself. There was nothing cruel about Callum's statement. And it was nothing she had not thought herself a hundred times since stepping foot over the gilded threshold of Penhallow. Nothing every single person here had not thought. Or voiced aloud.

You don't belong here.

Nothing which was not the simple truth.

After checking on Viola who was snoring thickly, Cat went for a long walk to clear her head. She climbed over fences and stepped around cows until the wind off the sea found her. It whipped through her hair and snapped her dress against her calves. The water boiled and frothed far below her, tiny ships already setting out in search of fish.

When she returned to the house and found herself in the bustling breakfast room, she felt more like herself. She had her equilibrium back. She didn't belong here because she belonged to the sea and the village and her dogs and most of all, her family. She would do anything for them. Steal from a duke. Drink tea from a cup as delicate as a seashell while Lady Siddal snickered in her direction. Luckily, Callum had not deigned to join them and so those particular slights slid off her like melted butter. She could ignore them when he was not there to give them weight. He was somewhere else, apparently talking to Mr. Armstrong.

Not ideal that.

Sunlight sparkled at the windows and over the silver cutlery as the guests helped themselves to a stunning selection of food. There was tea and coffee and marzipan in the shape of birds. Cream that dissolved like clouds in the warmed chocolate as it was poured into Cat's cup. Cat ate two scones with extra blackberry jam, coddled eggs, herbed potatoes, and fried trout. It was delicious and well worth the snide remarks about how ladies should eat like baby birds. They had clearly never eaten like baby birds and then set out to work a field or bring in the nets.

"I am not a bird," Summer said loudly, deliberately helping herself to another scone. "Nor do I aspire to be any such thing.

Three ladies and the vicar helped themselves to more pastries after noticing the flattering, interested look Lord Blackwood sent her way. For once she did not snap at him. She kept her attention on the pot of jam for an inordinately long time. He winked at Cat. She flashed him a grin, the kind her brother usually prompted from her.

"Right," Summer announced abruptly. "I hope you've eaten more than a bird would because we are off to the seaside. And you shall need your strength."

"Oh, I do love to paint the waves," Lady Siddal said. "Turner himself said I have a way to capturing them."

"Paint them?" Summer scoffed, setting down her linen napkin. A row of sapphires marched around her throat like raindrops. "Swimming, Lady Siddal. Today's task is swimming."

Lady Siddal blinked. "I thought that was a jest."

"Not at all," Summer sounded prim, but the effect was ruined by the gleam in her eye. "My brother takes swimming *very* seriously."

"But… is it very dangerous?" Lady Imogen asked tremulously.

"Only if you drown," Lady Ruby returned flatly. "So don't drown."

SUMMER LED THEM along a well trodden path through the long grass. Steps carved into the cliff led them down to a secluded cove, private to the family. There was no danger of spying eyes or the stench of a pilchard harvest off the beach. Footmen carried hampers of towels and food and laid them out on the warm rocks before departing. Three maids waited in the shadow of the cliff.

The sun warmed smooth stones and sand underfoot, hillocks of grass dotted with wildflowers, and sparkled off the water. The waves murmured and whispered secrets to the ladies milling around uncertainly. The tide pool was one of the largest Cat had ever seen, surrounded on all sides by smooth stone, like melted beeswax. The movements of the tide filled the crater and then retreated, leaving it to be warmed by the sun. During such a hot spell of weather, it would feel like bathwater.

She remembered it well.

Lady Summer was not cruel enough to force them into the cold sea, though Cat wondered if she might steal a moment to do just that. The push of water as you struggled to keep upright was invigorating and would bring her solidly back to her body. She'd been in her head entirely too much.

Work needed doing. It was time to be a village girl.

"A show of hands from the strong swimmers, please?" Summer called out. Cat, Lady Ruby, Miss Wentworth raised their hands. "Excellent. Ladies, you are in the best of care so no need to be alarmed. And it's not very deep around the edges."

"I don't have a swimming dress," Lady Imogen fretted, her cheeks already pinkening with the sun. She was all cream and sugar. "And there are no bathing machines!"

"This isn't Brighton," Lady Ruby rolled her eyes, though her tone was not unkind. "And you're not going into the sea, only the pool."

"It's like a bath," Cat assured her.

"In Brighton, they have dippers," Lady Imogen frowned.

"I have no intention of being dipped like a candle into the ocean," Summer said.

"But… those ladies are very strong. What if I slip and go under?"

"Miss Sparrow is a *sturdy* girl, "Lady Siddal remarked. Cat knew exactly what she meant by sturdy. Too soft, too wide, too curved. Too strong.

"Statuesque," Summer agreed. "Just as my brother prefers," she added archly.

Cat smiled weakly at Summer's outrageous and incendiary comment. Someone was likely to hold her head under if Summer didn't stop.

Lady Siddal sniffed. "I suppose a village girl who sings shanties would know everything about swimming and seaweed and fish." Her disdain was palpable, her smile all teeth. "One can smell it on you, after all."

"You can stand by me," Cat said to Lady Imogen, because it was safer than anything else she might have said in the moment. "I won't let you go under."

"Thank you," Lady Imogen's lips trembled. She reminded Cat of the kittens Cook was harboring, bumbling on soft feet, anxious and always seeking comfort. Lady Imogen dropped her voice to a whisper. "I still don't have a bathing dress."

"Neither do I," Cat admitted. She'd never needed one. You swam in your chemise or in the nude. A special dress made to soak up water and pull you under seemed like madness to her.

"You shan't need one," Summer announced. "We'll be perfectly fine in our chemises." There was a pause. "Come on ladies, no simpering misses here. Gwyn, Mary and Isolde are here to assist us."

There was a flurry of activity as the ladies' maids lent their assistance with buttons and ties and the laces of stays. Cat had never had a maid as her short stays laced in the front. The tense, hesitant atmosphere gradually gave way as the ladies stepped into the warm water. Muscles softened, shoulders loosened. And though the stress of such an odd competition did not dissolve, it was slightly overpowered by the pleasures of a late summer's day.

Lady Imogen stuck close to Cat, but after a few minutes of not dying a terrible watery death, she too relaxed. Summer swam lazily in the clear green water, her dark hair piled on top of her head. Cat might not be a dipper, but she found herself assisting the women who could not swim well as they gravitated towards her. Cat didn't mind. She needed something to distract her.

Because she remembered this tide pool. Vividly.

How could she not?

She had swum here once, a very long time ago, with a young Callum, not yet the duke, not even quite a man yet. They peeled their clothes off and slipped into the water, legs brushing, fingers touching, breaths meeting in the evening air above their heads. When he'd kissed her, every thought, every worry had fled. She'd never had a moment like that before or since. She was a woman who could barely afford the roof over her family's head, with a sister who wanted more, a brother who was not meant for the dangers of fishing, and too many dogs to feed. Worry was like air. She knew it more intimately than she had ever known Callum.

But not that night. She still remembered the way he'd dragged her through the water towards him, his hands strong and purposeful, his dark eyes burning. Before his father died, before he became a duke. Before everything changed.

"All right, ladies. The Duchess Games continue!"

Summer's voice cut through her daydream. It was probably best not to think about Callum. About what they might have been to each other. About the way she sometimes caught him looking at her in the drawing room and the heat that chased through her in response.

Lady Imogen perched comfortably on a smooth stone outcrop, her legs making circles under the water. "I think I shall forfeit this race."

Summer raised an eyebrow. "Very bold."

Lady Imogen flushed as though she had been offered the best of compliments. "Anyone else?"

"Certainly not," Lady Siddal said, surprising no one. She floated like a leaf, delicate and elegant. There was nothing hesitant about her.

In the end it was down to Lady Siddal, Lady Ruby, Miss Wentworth, Miss Emmeline, and Cat. The pool was just wide enough to accommodate them. Cat's heart bumped its rhythm. She might not be as competitive as her sister, but she owned she did not wish to lose to Lady Siddal and her belittling sneers. She wised Viola were here. She'd have already won the race and would be sitting daintily at the finish line wearing a crown of wildflowers.

But alas. It was down to Cat to save the family name.

In so many more ways than this. A twinge of unease went through her. This race meant nothing, really. But it *felt* heavy and sharp, nonetheless. Like a foreshadowing. If she could not win a simple swimming race, how could she run a smuggling gang? How could save her siblings?

The water lapped at her neck, tauntingly. How could—

"Miss Sparrow! *Swim!*"

She was only a second or two behind, but she'd been so trapped in her own thoughts, she hadn't heard Summer shout "Begin!" It was Lady Imogen screaming Cat's name in a screech worthy of any fishwife that set Cat to moving. She pumped her legs, sliced her arms through water. All she could see were bubbles, frothing waves, a slice of blue sky above. The tide pool churned with the force of their swimming, pushing, pushing. Someone cursed. Loudly. The race ended abruptly in gasps for air and bursts of laughter.

Summer stood on the edge of the pool, red-cheeked from shouting encouragements. "And it's a tie! Congratulations, Lady Siddal... and Miss Sparrow!"

Never mind the revenue men.

A pack of aristocratic ladies would stab her with their diamond hairpins long before.

Chapter Fourteen

CAT ELECTED TO stay on the beach a little longer after everyone else returned to the house. The maids helped the others on with their gowns, the footmen returned for the hampers of wet towels. She was finally alone and able to breathe again as she walked into the softly churning sea. She was unaccustomed to maids and their polite, distant eyes on her all the day long, to footmen and butlers and housekeepers. To aristocrats in any number and certainly in *such* numbers. She missed her quiet kitchen in the morning—if not the dozens of tasks that was required of her. She missed her dogs.

The sea washed away the worst of the anxious worries, of her thoughts looping on themselves, fueling a tremble in her chest, like she had stepped off an extra stair without realizing it. The drop of her stomach, the tilt of the world around, the slam into reality. Honestly, it was exhausting.

Here, for a blessed long moment, she only had to tilt against the waves, not the entire world. She wouldn't win, of course, water always won. But at least there was joy in this kind of fight. Exhilaration. The cold water stole her breath when she plunged into a wave, and she came up grinning. Gulls wheeled overhead, shouting at her when they realized she had no crumbs, no fish guts, nothing but appreciation for their flight. You couldn't eat appreciation.

Refusing to let her thoughts derail into darker territories, she let the waves push her to shore. The sun warmed the top of her head, water dripping from her heavy hair and the hem of her chemise.

It would have soaked her dress—if she still had a dress.

She rushed to the stone where she knew perfectly well she had left her folded dress, her stays and her stockings. Her shoes.

Nothing but sunlight and water dripping from her hair onto the stone.

Someone had stolen her clothing.

She was stunned for a full minute before anger shimmered through her. She couldn't prove it was Lady Siddal's doing of course, but she didn't know anyone else with that kind of petty dislike. And she had been rather vexed to have tied with a "fishing girl." Cat looked down at her wet chemise which was shockingly transparent. She couldn't be seen like this. Bad enough when it was dry, but it was positively indecent in this condition.

With a sigh, she stretched out on a smooth stone ridge around the pool and let the sun dry her as best it could. It was warm and quiet, and she drowsed despite herself. When she woke fully to a gull complaining very loudly near her ear, her chemise was damp but passable.

Best get to it.

She climbed the cliff steps and poked her head up before moving to the grassy path. No one and nothing but fields and the house in the distance. She knew from her morning walk that she could dart around the side garden, climb over the stone wall, and pop through one of the side servant doors with none the wiser.

The only tricky part was crossing the gravel walk at the edge of the formal hedges. It was more open than she liked. Someone might spy her from the house or if they were taking a turn around the garden. She reminded herself that she did not particularly care what the others thought about her, only about bringing in the next cargo. She felt a bit better and much worse.

She'd only been at Penhallow a few days and her whole sense

of self was turned upside down.

Well, not her *entire* character.

That fact became blazingly clear when she saw three ladies on the path. One of whom shrieked and kicked her foot out. It wasn't until Cat realized Lady Siddal had kicked Bartholomew the turtle that she felt fury. Not the inconvenience or embarrassment of a schoolroom prank that left her in the unmentionables. Not annoyance.

Fury.

She was her mother's daughter in that moment.

And definitely in the next, when Lady Siddal kicked the poor turtle again.

The first kick was no doubt out of fear, the second was anger. Luckily, Bartholomew was old and wide and made of sterner stuff. And luckily for Lady Siddal, he did not close his snapping jaw around her foot and chomp it like an apple. More's the pity. Instead, he pulled his head in sharply.

Cat did not realize she had moved or made any conscious decision until she had already launched herself at Lady Siddal. A village girl in her wet chemise seizing retribution for a turtle.

She never landed.

A strong arm banded around her midsection, seizing her from the air. Her wild battle yell strangled in her throat. Callum's chest pressed against her back. She'd know him anywhere, the smell of salt and wind and expensive spices.

"Ladies," he said starkly before hauling her away. She fought his hold like any wild creature, to no avail. Lady Siddal and the two other ladies gaped after them. Bartholomew trundled into the hedges, creating chaos and then deserting it, as usual.

"Let go," Cat said to Callum between her teeth.

He hefted her closer, tighter. His mouth was near her ear. "Not until you calm down."

She was struggling out of instinct, but there was something delicious about the solid warmth of him pressing against her. About the strength in his arms, his breath in her ear.

He went through a side door and then turned sharply, kicking open another door. They found themselves in an empty closet, the kind reserved for cloaks and beaver-brimmed hats during formal events.

"She kicked our turtle! She might have damaged his shell!" The moment he set her down, she whirled and went for the door.

It did not open.

Callum surged forward, large hand flattening against the door. "Settle," he growled. He towered over her, enveloped her. She struggled again, partly out of curiosity. Partly because being told to settle made her fume. He slid his leg between hers, edging them apart slightly, his boot planted against the door, holding it closed effortlessly. Her reaction was immediate, and very, very thorough. Heat chased down her spine, up her thighs. Warmth pulsed through her quim.

Behind her, his breath turned ragged. "Why are you damp? And… wearing that?"

It was hard to find her voice. She wanted to arch back against him like a cat. "Someone stole my clothes."

"I beg your pardon." The cold snap of his voice should have doused the lust moving through her.

It absolutely did not.

It was hard and unforgiving as ice, promising the same merciless end. Not against her but against anyone who might have harmed her. "Who?" he demanded.

"I can't be sure," she admitted.

"Mm-hmm." He didn't sound convinced. And he was closing the very tiny spaces left between their bodies, so it was difficult to concentrate. The perfect juxtaposition of Callum Winter and the Duke of Tremaine: fire and ice.

"She may have stolen my clothes, but I don't care about that. It's a petty tantrum. But she hurt a creature who posed no threat to her, Callum. That second kick was deliberate."

"I will handle it."

"I can handle it myself."

"Cat, if you assault a guest, my mother will drive you out of here with pitchforks and torches. She will shred your reputation."

"I don't care," she replied mutinously, even though she knew he was right. And that she should care. Her smuggling plans would certainly care.

"I care," Callum said darkly. "When will I have the chance to see you again? Even if only across a drawing room? It's been ten years." He sounded desperate, wrecked like a boat against the rocks. "Longer."

Something caught in her throat. Something suspiciously like want and need and wonder. "I didn't think you remembered that. Not really."

"Remember it?" He all but growled. "It's been the air I breathe."

She swallowed, aching all over. Stunned. Nervous. Desperate for this to be simpler than it was. "Callum."

"I've already stood up in front of God and country to sing a sea shanty like a lovesick fool," he muttered. "Don't let it be for naught. Not if this is all I ever get."

If she didn't turn around, if they didn't look each other in the eye, they could pretend this had never happened. That it meant nothing. Complicated nothing.

Because it meant everything. She knew it did. How could it not? And yet, she couldn't let it make a difference. Not outside this little room.

But *inside* this little room?

She shifted sightly, pressing back against the hardening of him. He groaned, both hands splayed against the door on either side of her head. His mouth touched her neck, teeth scraping. She made a little sound in the back of her throat. She couldn't help it. Tingles awoke under his lips and darted lower, right between her legs.

"Tell me to stop," he murmured against her skin.

"Absolutely not," she shot back before she could think of something much more sophisticated to say. Before she could remember all of the very good reasons why this was a very bad idea.

He smiled, flicking his tongue behind her ear until she thought she might melt. Or burst. She reached behind blindly, trying to bring him closer. She clutched at his hip. She was starting to feel a little wild. "Don't stop."

He trapped her wrists together in his left hand, keeping them still and pressing them to the door above her head. Everything about it made her wet. Desperate. So desperate.

Especially when he added, dark and gruff. "I thought I told you to settle."

"You'll have to try harder than that." She had no notion as to why she wanted to push back, wanted to tease and test until he made her gasp his name. Until they had no choice but to give in, despite logic and good sense.

Or why she liked it so much.

He stilled, briefly. His manhood twitched against her. His hands tightened. And then he chuckled, low and silky and every inch a duke who would be obeyed. Her thighs trembled.

"Is that so?" He ran his open mouth against her neck, nipping. He pressed harder against her and she had nowhere to go, no place for her worries or her plans. Not when his free hand grazed her waist, moved down her leg to snatch at the hem of her chemise just below her knees. He grabbed the material with force, as if it personally offended him. As if the very thought of it separating him from her was an affront.

His harsh breath in her ear drowned out her moans when his fingers grazed her, ever so gently. Teasing. Making her squirm to get closer. So much closer even though there wasn't even enough space left between them for a shaft of light. He kicked her ankles apart with his boot and she gasped. She was open to his hand now, to his long fingers that played over her so softly she pushed back against his erection. He laughed again, quietly. "Did you want something, Miss Sparrow?"

"Don't tease me. *Your Grace.*" She strained against him, trying to wriggle her pinned wrists free. To touch him. To push him over the edge so he would take her with him.

"Say please."

"*Callum.*"

He ran his fingertip between her folds, still barely touching her. Tauntingly close to her bud but never giving her what he knew she wanted. Want sharpened through her, muddling every thought that wasn't Callum's hands, Callum's tongue, Callum's thighs flexing against her. She clenched around nothing. He dipped into her slickness, a taunt. "I can't hear you, siren."

As if she was the one calling men to the depths of the ocean with a song. As if *he* wasn't the one threatening to drown her in want. "*Please.*"

"There," he said, as if she'd pleased him.

And then he slid two fingers into her, and she trembled with the sudden invasion, intimate muscles quivering. When his thumb finally, finally circled her bud, it sparked through her. She felt it in her stomach, in her thighs, in her throat as it worked around another moan, husky and startled. He kept whispering in her ear, each word ripped out of him as he brought her closer and closer to her climax. "You feel so good," he said, and she panted as his fingers crooked deep inside her. His voice was positively filthy, in the most beautiful way. "So hot and wet. I know just how you'll taste." He increased the rhythm of his fingers, steady, deep. "Divine."

She had never felt her body so keenly.

"You're going to come for me, aren't you, siren?"

It was building and building and just this side of too much.

"Come," he commanded softly, just as his teeth closed over the spot where her neck and shoulder met. "Now."

She didn't just come, she very nearly came apart. The spirals of sensations tightened and tightened and then loosed all at once. She slumped, her cheek pressed against the door, panting. Tiny tremors of aftershock pulsed through her.

He eased back and shrugged out of his coat. He placed it

around her shoulders, brushing his mouth gently, high on her cheekbone, before pulling the door open and slipping out of the closet without a word.

Chapter Fifteen

WITHOUT A WORD, mind you.

It was infuriating. And yet it made her just as hot all over as his stern and unyielding attention. And this way, they might pretend a little longer. Just a little longer.

He'd thought of her? After all this time?

Cat ran all the way up the servant stairs, praying no one would see her in her chemise and a gentleman's coat. Not just a gentleman's, but the duke's. Not to mention, she was fairly certain her cheeks were indecently pink. How could they not be with lust still sparking through her?

Voices lifted from the main stairs as guests sought their rooms for rest or to change before dinner. Servants' footsteps sounded down the other end of the hall. Panicked, Cat popped into the sitting room she shared with Viola as it was the closest door. She hoped fervently that her sister was still in bed as she did not know how to answer any of the questions that would no doubt start flying at her head. She needed a moment to think, to ground the memory of Callum inside her body where no one could ever take it away from her.

Of course, Viola was *not* in her bedroom.

Neither was she alone.

Worse yet, Lady Ruby was her visitor and Lady Ruby was entirely too sharp and perceptive for comfort. As evidenced by the immediate lifting of her eyebrows. "Is that the duke's coat?"

Cat froze. "Um."

Viola sat right up on the settee, her nose still pink but her eyes clear. "Cat, why are you in your chemise?"

"We went swimming."

Lady Ruby's eyes narrowed. "That was two hours ago."

"Yes," Cat sighed, dropping into a chair and reaching for tea from the tray. Thankfully, it was still hot. A large pot of honey sat next to it.

"The honey is for Miss Viola," Lady Ruby explained. She looked faintly shy for the first time. Almost as though she was trying not to blush. "It's mixed with horehound and licorice root."

"It tastes awful," Viola says cheerfully. "But it works."

"I'm glad," Cat said, adding lemon to her cup instead. She had the notion that Lady Ruby might actually slap her hand away if she dared try the honey. "You do look better."

"I haven't sneezed in nearly eighteen minutes."

Cat grinned. "Good, you were starting to sound like an angry donkey."

Viola stuck out her tongue. "You still haven't explained how you've lost your dress." She paused. Lady Ruby paused. They looked at each other, then at Cat. "Is it very salacious?"

Salacious didn't begin to cover it.

"Someone stole my dress," Cat explained flatly.

Viola scowled, the pretty sunshine of her face instantly turning to the kind of thundercloud that sank ships. "*What?*"

"Just a prank."

"A prank if you were still twelve years old."

"She's right," Lady Ruby said. "You could have been ruined."

Cat wrinkled her nose. "I might still be. Lady Siddal kicked Sir Bartholomew. *Twice.*"

"Who?" Lady Ruby asked, perplexed. "I have not met a Bartholomew. Has he just arrived?"

"He's a turtle."

"Oh no," Viola groaned. "*What* did you do, Cat?"

Cat sipped her tea primly. "I may have launched myself at her, using Mother's patented banshee attack."

Viola groaned again. "Bollocks." Their mother had once broken a magistrate's nose when he whipped his horse. Cat was still not sure how she had avoided being tossed into a jail cell. Her beauty no doubt softened the blow, as it often did. Viola had the same privilege, even pulling a face as she was now. "Still, Lady Siddal deserved it."

"She does have a beastly temper, "Lady Ruby murmured, watching them as if they were the most fascinating thing she had ever seen. She clearly had no sisters of her own.

And Lady Siddal absolutely did deserve it. But it was more than enough to get Cat kicked out of the house. But after Callum's voice in her ear and his fingers playing her like a lute, part of her hoped she'd be marched off the premises by several burly footmen. She couldn't betray him then.

She couldn't save her family either.

"And Lady Siddal doesn't like that you're winning," Lady Ruby added.

Cat's laugh was more of a startled bark. "Don't be ridiculous."

"Viola, one point. Watercolors, point to me. Singing, Swimming, two points to Cat."

"My sea shanty did not win the challenge," Cat scoffed. "I played *the spoons*."

"And the duke rose from his chair to sing with you."

"Did he?" Viola turned towards her slowly. "You never said."

"It was nothing."

"And now you wear his coat." Lady Ruby really was relentless.

Cat sighed, suddenly tired. "Let's be realistic, if you please. I could win every challenge from here to Judgement Day and I still would not be a duchess."

Viola didn't reply but she narrowed her eyes in a way that

Cat couldn't quite interpret. Cat narrowed her eyes back on principle. Then she stuck out her tongue.

"Very duchess-like," Viola snorted.

"See? I told you."

"I'll leave you both to rest." Lady Ruby didn't know what to make of them. That much was obvious. Still, when she stood it was somewhat reluctantly. "That's very pretty lace," she said noticing the piece Cat had yet to sew onto her dinner dress. "I hardly ever see such pretty work these days. My modiste would kill to have such stock again."

Cat did not look at her sister. Her sister did not look at her. "Viola makes it herself."

Ruby glanced at Viola's hands. They weren't the soft hands of a lady, but nor did they have calluses from lace bobbins. She was not naturally stooped, after hours hunched over delicate work. Only another woman who knew of such things would notice. Mr. Armstrong would have no clue. Cat had no doubt Lady Ruby was far more intelligent than ten revenue men. "Does she now?"

Viola just nodded.

"Your work is very French."

"Thank you. And thank you for the honey," Viola said softly. Lady Ruby nodded and turned away without saying anything else. Viola watched her leave. "I think she might be lonely."

"Do you?" She might also be a candidate to help Cat move her contraband lace to London. She suddenly liked the other woman enormously. It was a risk, of course. But everything was.

"She's really very nice. Much nicer than I thought at first. She's just prickly, like a hedgehog." Viola collected hedgehogs. She had a way with them. She snuggled back against the cushions. "I think she wants the thrill of winning the competition more than she wants the actual duke."

"And you?"

Don't say you want Callum. Please, don't say you want Callum.

Not that it mattered in the end.

"I'd like never to have to eat pilchard again."

Relief, however short-lived flowed through her.

She dipped her finger into the honey now that Lady Ruby wasn't here to stop her. "A love sonnet, if I ever heard one."

CAT, WISELY, DID not descend to dinner that night.

She took a supper tray in the sitting room with Viola, not wanting to have any more of the dowager duchess's attention on her. Or anyone's for that matter. Lady Imogen's father had taken to baring his teeth at her. It was disconcerting. And not just because he'd earlier bragged that two of them were taken from brave soldiers who died fighting the French.

She went out into the gardens as soon as the sun had set and crawled around under the library window.

Where she found mushrooms, pebbles, a hawk feather—and no ducal ring.

It was already gone.

Had a gardener found it? A helpful guest?

Did Callum remember her pointing out the hawk's nest?

Did he suspect her at all?

Chapter Sixteen

THE NEXT MORNING Cat went home.

Mostly to reassure herself that her brother was safe, her animals cared for, and her cellars undiscovered. They might be empty but hopefully that wouldn't be the case for much longer.

Sleep eluded her as usual. But this time, between bouts of fretting, she couldn't stop remembering the feel of Callum pressing against her. The things he'd said to her. The things he'd done to her. It was a mistake to replay them in her head, over and over until she was squirming with need. A mistake, but utterly impossible to avoid.

As was Callum, himself.

She dressed, wound her hair in a knot and traded her one pair of good shoes for her usual boots. Matthew was nearly a man grown and could no doubt take care of himself, but he wouldn't bother with proper meals, just a hunk of bread stuffed in his pocket so he could race off to the blacksmith. The anvil and the blacksmith's daughter held equal appeal. He probably hadn't eaten properly since she'd left. He most certainly hadn't weeded the cabbages.

And it would be hours before anyone else was up and about, never mind ready for whatever torture the dowager duchess had devised. It would be something suitably refined, meant to put Cat firmly back into her place. As many times as was necessary.

Cat was quite sure there would be no village lottery for the next event held at Penhallow. Noblesse Oblige wasn't meant to be such a nuisance.

"There's a smile for the devil himself," Callum said drily from right behind her.

Startled, Cat tried to punch him in the throat.

Hard.

He didn't bother dodging, only caught her fist before it connected with any part of his anatomy. Her heart raced and leapt right into her throat where it contemplated taking up permanent residence. She made a strange sound, somewhere between a laugh and a yelp.

"Miss Sparrow," he said calmly, just this side of stern. He was wearing a magnificently embroidered waistcoat. She was wearing a dress with a mended patch under the right arm. He raised an eyebrow.

Every part of her went hot and needy.

She swallowed a curse and attempted to school her features into something normal and not like a woman trying not to salivate. Honestly. It was embarrassing. And she'd been humiliated enough. "Your Grace." Her voice squeaked slightly but that at least could be attributed to getting caught trying to plant a duke a facer.

"I don't think fisticuffs are on the agenda for these blasted games," he said. His blue eyes turned to tarnished silver. Mesmerizing and filled with secrets. A veritable pirates' hoard.

She never used to be so fanciful. It was probably not a good sign. Next, she'd follow a will-o'-the-wisp and fall into a bog.

The fact that anyone, especially the sophisticated Lady Siddal, could feel threatened by her, a fisherman's daughter turned bog witch, was laughable.

"Caitriona."

She'd gotten lost in her thoughts again. Bollocks. She knew the sound of someone having said her name more than once. Callum was patient, with none of the exasperation she was accustomed to. It was comforting.

She could not let it be comforting.

"I'm sorry," she said finally. "You startled me."

He had not let go of her. His hand moved to circle her wrist. The image of him pinning her to the door slammed into her. Her toes curled in their worn, practical boots. She could feel his mouth on her neck, his fingers on her thighs. She tried to tug free, cheeks pinkening. He did not immediately allow it. She swallowed. "Callum?"

He dropped her hand.

She shouldn't have said anything. She missed his touch instantly. The warm strength of it. The promise in it.

"What are you doing out here?" he demanded as though she had snuck out in the dead of night with the family silver.

To be fair, she had every intention of robbing him.

She glanced at his fingers. He wore no ring. Had he chosen not to wear it? Or was it still missing? She couldn't very well ask him. Callum watched her. She'd waited too long to reply again. "I'm going home."

He frowned. "You're letting them drive you away?"

She blinked at the flash of fury under his usual control. Not at her. But at who? The house party? His own society? "No. Not yet anyway."

"Good girl," he murmured.

She blinked again. Why had those innocuous little words wrapped around her like silk? He didn't look at her, merely kept pace at her side. And he hadn't sounded condescending. Because she was fairly certain if anyone else had said that to her she would have landed that punch. Twice. So why then, when he said it, did her thighs press together involuntarily?

A kingfisher flew behind him, a flash of turquoise and copper feathers. The wind wound around her legs, ruffled the tall grass. "Where are *you* going?" she asked.

"Anywhere but here," he muttered.

She nibbled on her lower lip. "Did you want to come with

me?"

Caitriona Sparrow. A duke does not want to come to your cottage that smells of wet dog.

He paused, gaze sliding towards her. "I would, yes."

Oh.

She hadn't expected that. Even during that forbidden summer so long ago he had been careful not to come to her house. There would be too much gossip.

They walked in companionable silence, climbing down the road towards Little Crumpet. The sea was a constant backdrop, the sun flashing on the water, the tiny white specks of boats in the distance. The cottage sat on the edge of the village, which she loved. It was quiet and she could open the door and let the dogs out for a run even late at night. It came into view as they crested a hill, the thatched roof which had seen better days, the white-washed walls. They'd painted the windowsills a bright red for a bit of cheer. There were too many feelings welling up inside her, it was hard to sort them out: pride, embarrassment, nerves, confusion.

So, she did what she always did when the worry threatened to make her hands shake or her breath stutter. She moved. Action always helped. Laughter was even better. She tucked a strand of hair that had been pulled loose by the wind behind her ear. "It occurs to me that these Duchess Games are rather unfair."

"It occurs to you *now?*" He stopped walking because she had. "They're not unfair, they're downright ghoulish."

"True," she flashed him a grin. "But they are also uneven. We show off for you, but when do you show off for us?"

He raised an eyebrow, waiting. Usually, a duke's very presence was enough.

"I propose a race," she added. "A footrace."

"You want me to race you?"

She had flummoxed him. Good. It was high time he felt as unmoored as she did.

"Are you ready?" she asked. "Good. *Go!*" She tossed over her shoulder.

"I never said I—*damnation*."

Her laugh trailed behind her as he broke into a run. She was fast and she knew the path well. But he'd grown up walking the beaches and wading into the waves. Riding horses. Pugilism. Still, she hadn't expected someone so big to move quite so fast.

It was quickly apparent that she had miscalculated.

This was supposed to be a spot of silly fun, something to defuse the tension. She hadn't counted on the primal breathlessness he evoked by closing in behind her, his footsteps approaching, his shadow at her heels. Hunting her.

Did everything the man did have to make her feel as though he'd already taken all of her clothes off?

She pushed a little harder. He kept close. She felt the pounding of his boots in the ground. Yellow finches erupted out of the grass around them. Her neck prickled, even as she suppressed an inappropriate giggle. The cottage garden loomed, the wall snaking around it. She risked a backward glance at him, and the laugh died in her throat, replaced by a whimper of need. There was nothing polite in his expression, only intensity and smug satisfaction and the same kind of need that drove her. She could all but taste it.

He was running her to ground and she was loving it.

She reached the wall first. At least, she thought she reached it first. It was hard to tell when he was suddenly there and his hands were on her and she was spinning around, her back hitting the stones. They struggled for breath, eyes locked together. The morning spun away, the sun through the clouds, the call of herring gulls, the smell of the rosemary plants nearby. None of it mattered.

It took an eternity for their mouths to meet. He paused there for so long, teasing them both. When she finally closed the distance between them, touching her mouth to his gently, a nip here, a nibble. There was no softness in his response.

Only hunger.

His fingers closed in her hair, tilting her head back and anchoring it so he could find his pleasure. Which was her pleasure. He kissed her deeply, hungrily, chasing the whimpers she made against his mouth. Every sound of pleasure made his fingers flex. The sting of her scalp kept her in the moment.

He flattened his other hand to the small of her back, dragging her closer. The hardness of him thrilled her, thighs flexing against hers, muscled chest pebbling her nipples, cock nudging between her legs. The answering pull of heat made her squirm against him. His tongue touched hers again and again, a taste, a retreat, another taste. She didn't know how much more she could take. She hated every stitch of clothes between them.

"Are you wet for me, Miss Sparrow?"

She moaned against his mouth but when she didn't otherwise answer he pulled back, just slightly. She pressed forward, moaning again, insisting.

"Answer the question, Caitriona." His voice was rough against her ear, demanding, teasing. His teeth followed, a gentle scrape along the side of her throat. "There are rules."

She shivered. "Y-yes."

"Are you sure?" He tugged her lower lip into his mouth, soothed the sting with his tongue. His hands fisted in the material of her dress. She nodded, half frantic. "Prove it."

She slid her hand between their bodies, but instead of lifting her skirts as he expected, she palmed his erection instead. "You first," she said. She wanted to undo the buttons of his breeches. With her teeth. "Prove how hard you are for me."

A soft graze at first, just enough for him to still, and then she stroked him harder until his breath hissed out. Who was she? How did he make her feel both so wild and so safe that she could make outrageous demands. Power and surrender twined inside of her.

"You wish me to prove it, do you?" he asked, fitting his body to hers and driving forward. His cock pressed deeper against her softness, heedless of breeches and skirts and the fact that anyone might walk down the road and glance their way. She gasped, rubbing along his length until he cursed. "I want to—"

A loud bark, followed by much louder, much more frenzied barking.

The dogs had realized someone was lurking in the back of the garden. There was a howl, just bordering on hysterical. Impossible to ignore. Percival had realized it was her. He would chew through the walls to get to her.

Callum dropped his forehead to hers. "Is your brother likely to send them out to tear me from limb from limb?"

She smiled, apologetically. "Yes."

"Might be worth it." He kissed her again, just once but it was hard and possessive in a way she would not have thought she would like so much.

"Callum?" she said as they broke apart.

"Yes?"

"I still won the footrace."

His soft startled laugh followed her all the way around to the front door of the cottage.

Chapter Seventeen

CALLUM LOVED SPARROW cottage.

It was small and full of dogs and the gentle clutter of an actual home, not a mausoleum to a line of dead dukes going back practically to the bloody Battle of Hastings. More, it kept Cat safe and warm and dry and for that alone he would have gilded it as a monument. It did all of the things he was desperate to do and could not. Not properly.

She would never let him.

She seemed nervous as she led him inside. It was too hot for a fire in the grate, so the wooden table was pulled in front of it, piled with bowls of berries, a heel of bread wrapped in cloth, two empty cups.

"Matthew?" Cat called out even as three monsters fell upon her barking and whining with hysterical joy. If he hadn't already known they were dogs, he might have considered them beasts charging out of some fairy tale. Their heads reached her collarbone, even with all four paws on the floor. She laughed, staggering to hold her balance. Callum placed his hand against her lower back to keep her steady.

"I was gone for a few days," she protested, evading a happy lick from a tongue the size of a ham. "Percival, down." Percival snuffled against her adoringly. Three long whips of tails wagged back and forth, knocking over a basket of knitting, a candle and a cup. Cat just laughed again. "Alright, you monsters, back. Pretend you have manners."

At the command "manners," all three dogs sat. Callum was impressed. An older black dog of indeterminate breed lifted his head from a cushion. His gray muzzle was very dignified. He'd seen royalty with less dignity. "This is King Arthur," Cat said, stepping over to pat his head. Of course. "He's in charge."

"Naturally."

"And this is Guinevere and her pups, Merlin and Percival. The rest of the menagerie is outside."

"There's more?" He looked around. He couldn't imagine fitting three humans and four dogs in the cottage. Where did she sleep? He frowned at the straw mattress tucked in the back corner, behind a screen.

"Matthew?" Cat called out, gathering dirty dishes as she went. He wasn't sure she even noticed. He could see a different kind of confidence—and weariness—in her. He wanted to send his entire household staff, all seventy-seven of them, down to sweep the floors, bake the bread, do whatever it was Cat clearly did to keep house for a small zoo on what must be pennies. He would have Cook pack several baskets and send them by carriage. And he'd send a real bed, damn it. She could curse him all she liked. It was as good as done. He might have a word with her brother as well, for letting his older sister sleep on the floor.

Footsteps sounded from the loft above. Cat looked up and called out, louder this time. "Wake up, slugabed."

Matthew's head poked over the ladder. He was young, his hair mussed, his expression confused. "Cat? What are you doing here?"

"I came to check on you."

A snort. "You came to check on your dogs."

"True."

Matthew gave a start when he spotted Callum. He stopped, mid-yawn. "Who's that?"

"This is His Grace."

"Go on with 'ee."

Cat glanced at Callum, then snickered at her brother. "No, really."

"Oh." He blinked rapidly, looking uncomfortable. More than uncomfortable. There was panic there, stuffed behind the bravado of a seventeen-year-old boy. "I should put on pants."

Caitriona rolled her eyes. The footsteps above them picked up speed.

And doubled.

Matthew wasn't alone. Poor girl. She was likely mortified. Callum moved his gaze to the window out of courtesy.

"Why don't I show you the goat," Cat blurted out.

Through the wavy glass, he caught the unmistakable shape of a young man dropping from the loft window and fleeing through the garden in his underwear.

Cat froze. The worry came off of her in waves. Percival pressed his giant nose in her palm. "You don't want to see a goat," she said quickly. "How about some tea?"

Callum shifted, his expression turning cold and ducal, hiding any real feelings behind the façade of a dignified Tremaine. Their mother had demanded that of him practically since birth. He was grateful for it for the first time in his life because it meant he did not betray a hint that he had seen anything. Not even when Matthew threw himself down the ladder at a breakneck pace and Cat turned on her heel with a wide, distracting smile, placing herself between him and her brother. Protecting him.

Callum wanted to tell her she never had anything to fear from him. Ever. For any reason. He would have if he'd thought she'd believe him. But he knew she would feel better if she thought he hadn't noticed anything. Truthfully, he could not have cared less where her brother found his pleasure. But he understood why she looked ready to do battle with a minotaur. There were those who would see young Matthew severally punished. Hurt. Outright murdered over it. And those black-guards would have an unjust law at their behest.

All that mattered to Callum was Cat. And her happiness.
Period.

Matthew ran a hand over his hair, smiling ruefully. His cheeks were red. "Apologies, Your Grace."

"No need," Callum said. "I'm in your home unexpectedly. And rather early."

Matthew snorted. "Cat doesn't sleep." She pinched him. "Ouch. What?"

"You're not supposed to talk about sleeping," she hissed.

"I was talking about not-sleeping."

"Well, that too."

"I haven't even pissed yet, Cat. The sun's barely up. It's too early to scold me." He frowned. "Now what? Why are you so red in the face?"

"You're not supposed to talk about bodily functions either."

"Well, that's stupid."

"He's right," Callum said.

Cat blinked, surprised. He didn't blame her. The entire mask and shield of his persona as the duke relied on the rules her brother just maligned. But even with the hidden panic and the embarrassment Cat tried to hide, this cottage was already warmer than his estate had ever been. She'd scoff and think him an idiot, but he'd trade a hundred gold candlesticks for dog fur on the chairs and ale spills on the table. Even as he thought it, she wiped at it hastily with a cloth, shooting her brother daggers.

"Percival did it with his tail," he said.

She turned slowly. "Are you blaming my dog?"

"That thing is a menace."

"That *thing* will piss on your bed if I ask him to."

Matthew grinned. "I thought we weren't supposed to talk about that."

She threw the cloth at his head. Callum stood stiff and formal, hands held behind his back as though he were in the army. He knew he looked unapproachable. But he felt as though he'd swallowed the entire sun and he didn't know what to do with his face. This was the Cat he knew, the Cat he remembered from that summer. Laughing, irreverent, spirited. He hated the cold etiquette of his house and title, and he hated them even more when they strangled her. She was too good for the disdain and the power plays. The gossip. The pranks.

That, at the very least, had been dealt with.

While he yearned and called himself ten times a fool for being here when he should stay far, far away, Cat interrogated Matthew about her dogs. If they were eating, if they had tried to take over the butcher shop again. About her goat. And what he thought might be a one-winged parrot in a cage covered over with cloth. His language was *not* proper. *"Bollocks to you!"*

Mathew choked on a laugh. Cat poked him with her elbow, also trying not to laugh. He wanted his mouth on hers again, to feel that curve against his lips. The way her breath trembled against him. "Apologies," Cat said. "Your Grace."

"Bollocks to Your Grace!"

His mouth twitched against a smile when she snorted a laugh. She stared at him, as if transfixed, then looked hastily away.

"Percival breaks out at least three times a day no matter what I do," Matthew complained. "He keeps looking for you."

Cat ruffled his fur. "Poor fellow," she said as he pressed against her adoringly. "He's still a bit young," she explained to Callum. "And he was the skinniest when we found him."

"He sleeps under the blankets with her," Matthew added. "And he hasn't left her side since."

"He's a good boy."

"He's a menace when he doesn't know where you are," he grumbled. "He ate my left boot."

"And what have *you* eaten since I left? And ale doesn't count as food."

"Alice brought me a stargazy pie last night." Matthew nodded to the dish tucked against the stones where it would stay cool. It was a pie made with eggs and potatoes, with sardines kept whole, their heads poking up through the crust. "Would you like a piece?" he asked politely.

"I don't think a duke wants stargazy pie," Cat said dubiously.

"I disagree," Callum said, forcing his posture to relax. To not be menacing. He was probably only half successful. "I happen to like stargazy pie."

She blinked. "You do?"

"I do." When he was nineteen, the Huer's wife had brought it to him for months, to thank him for taking over for her husband when he had to rush home when her birthtime came early. All he'd done was stand on the cliff and wave gorse branches and shout. It was meant to let the village know that a shoal of pilchard had been spotted. He'd tried to refuse the gift of the pie, and she'd looked so crestfallen that instead he'd eaten the whole thing standing right there. It tasted better than all the lobster sauce and white soup his mother insisted they eat.

That was before his father died. Before he became a duke. Before everything changed.

It tasted better still at Cat's worn and dented kitchen table while sitting in a chair with a slightly frayed wicker back that kept poking him in the kidney.

"I've got a Figgy 'Obbin too," Matthew offered.

"Who brought you that?" Cat asked.

"The baker's daughter."

"Of course, she did. She thinks you hung the moon." She turned to Callum. "Have you tried it? It's like a sweet pasty stuffed with raisins." She wrinkled her nose. "I don't suppose there's a lot of Figgy 'Obbin in London."

"Figgy 'Obbin is my favorite." He knew the exact moment she recalled the first time he'd ever had it. Straight from her hand while they sat in the tide pool and licked sugar off each other's lips. Her cheeks went pink. "Well, second favorite."

She didn't ask him what his favorite was.

Just as well.

He couldn't very well tell her *she* was his favorite sweet.

He could still taste her, from that long ago summer, from this morning by the garden wall. Taste her skin, her moans. He ate another mouthful of pastry to keep his hands from reaching for her. His hands didn't belong to a duke. They didn't care about propriety.

When it was time to return to Penhallow, Cat hugged her brother. "Be careful," she murmured pointedly.

"You don't have to check up on me, Cat."

"I'm checking up on the dogs," she nudged him. "I like them better." She made the rounds, offering scratches and praise.

Percival crammed himself in the doorway, blocking her. She kissed his enormous head. "I'm sorry, my fine knight. I have to go."

He whined once. She swallowed, visibly steeled herself. "Percival."

He whined again. Just once more but it was deeply pathetic. Cat winced.

That did it.

"Bring him."

"Truly? Are you sure?"

The way Cat looked at him made him want to have every dog in Cornwall brought to his house. Immediately.

"I'm sure."

Chapter Eighteen

CAT OPENED HER mouth to thank him but before she could say a single word every dog on the premises erupted into loud, furious barking. The dogs running outside, the dogs at her feet. Selkie, the tiny mongrel down the way. Even her goat by the back shed made some very unpleasant threatening noises.

"What in the—"

Cat went to open the door, but it rattled off its hinges before she could reach it.

Three revenue men, armed with muskets and cudgels, marched into the cottage, bristling with bravado and righteousness. New men to the post.

Bollocks.

King Arthur lunged. Matthew tried to stop him, missed. Cat shoved him with her leg, knocking him off his trajectory, terrified one of the men might shoot him. They deserved his teeth in their arse but he did not deserve the retribution that would surely follow. He jostled the table and three cups fell to the ground, shattering. Guinevere advanced, her puppies threatened.

"God's teeth!" One of the guns swung towards her.

"Guinevere, stay!" Cat shouted.

She moved to stand in front of her and the tallest of the agents barked: "No one moves! We are here on order of His Majesty the King!"

Matthew grabbed the fire poker.

It was absolute chaos.

Until the moment one of the agents pointed his musket at Cat.

"Enough." Callum's command rent the air like a cannon ball.

She'd never seen anything like it. He barely raised his voice, but it may as well have shaken the rafters. There was no question of disobedience. The dogs froze. Matthew gaped. The agents turned as one. "Who the hell are you?"

"I'm the Duke of Tremaine," Callum snapped. "And you'll get that gun away from the lady or you'll eat it."

The gun lowered. The agents, fired up for a righteous fight, blinked at each other, confused.

"State your purpose," Callum continued. He was every bit the duke, carved from marble. His face was hard, chiseled. His eyes had all the softness of slate. And somehow, he'd stepped between her and the agents without her realizing it. His arm went across her, his hand on her hip, keeping her tucked safely behind him.

"We're here on order of His Majesty the King?" the tallest repeated, but this time it came out as a question.

"To terrorize a woman and a boy?"

Matthew bristled. Cat shot him a warning glance. Better to be underestimated.

Because someone had sent these men to her door.

Juro.

She'd bet her share of the cargo on it. Damn the man. If they used the revenue men against each other in this way, only the revenue men won in the end.

"We were given a tip about contraband."

"About my cottage?" Cat asked. She tried to step around Callum but he wouldn't let her. She might have fought him on principle, but it was better if these men thought her scared and confused. It stuck like vinegar in her throat. She blinked innocently. "Sir, if I had contraband I would be living in a much grander house, don't you think?"

"Get out," Callum snapped. "And tell Armstrong I want to talk to him."

"Wait," Cat said, an idea taking hold. A bad idea. But in the long run, it might do her good. "They're only doing their duty."

Callum glanced down at her. "What?"

"I would hate for them to get into trouble," she continued. Would it be too much if she fluttered her eyelashes? She'd probably look like a bewildered goose. "I'm sure there's been some sort of mistake, but wouldn't it be best to let them search the cottage to clear things up?"

A risk. All of her hiding spots were empty but if they found the trapdoor under her mattress, it would engender questions. On the other hand, if they searched and found nothing, they would remember how accommodating she was. That she had the trust of a duke and was still willing to have her belongings tossed. If her name came up again, they'd be far more likely to disregard it. She would need that. Because the next time they searched there would be plenty to find.

The agents straightened their spines, as if she was their commanding officer. "You're very kind, miss."

"Mmh." Callum did not sound convinced. He mostly sounded disgruntled. She could have sworn he nodded companionably at King Arthur when he growled again.

"If you'll just let me take the dogs out," she said, touching King Arthur's collar. He subsided, but he didn't like it.

They stepped aside as she ushered four very suspicious dogs past them into the yard. Matthew was still in his smalls, frowning. "Can I put some pants on?"

The agents looked at each other, then at Callum. He inclined his head.

"Very well," the agent who fancied himself in charge said. "But be quick about it."

Matthew went up the ladder and they busied themselves lifting every cushion, every basket, every jug. They poked inside her knitting basket, tapped the walls with the ends of their cudgels. Cat watched them, taking careful notes as to where they searched so as to choose any future hiding spots more carefully. They approached her trunk of dresses. It was an odd, not terribly good feeling to watch strangers paw through her meager collection of stockings and stays. One of them toed her mattress.

She forced herself not to jump forward, not start babbling to distract them from the trapdoor hidden underneath. Not to act *guilty*.

"You'll be careful with her belongings," Callum ordered. "And courteous."

He stepped back. "Yes, sir."

"*Your Grace.*"

"Yes, Your Grace."

It didn't take them long to search the cottage, it was small, and they didn't have a lot of decorative clutter. There were seashells in the walls and hanging on strings. A few candles, a bowl of blackberries gathered from the hedges. Their dirty plates from stargazy pie and Figgy 'Obbin. The red ribbon a smitten boy had once given Viola.

"Nothing here," the first agent said. "Begging your pardon, Miss. We have to investigate every tip."

She nodded. "Of course, you do."

"If you're quite finished?" Callum cut in, coldly.

"Yes, Your Grace."

"Off with you."

They bowed smartly and left in haste. Cat released her breath. Matthew dropped into a chair, visibly sweating.

"Does that happen often?" Callum frowned.

She shook her head. "It's never happened before."

"And it will never happen again."

Chapter Nineteen

"THANK YOU," CAT said some time later when they left the cottage. She had adrenaline in her blood, a giant wolfhound at her heels and a duke at her side. She sent him a sidelong glance. "I thought you supported the revenue men."

"Naturally," he replied. "I might support the Crown, as required by my title, but I won't have them trampling through your house."

There was still a kindness to him, under all of that *duke*-ness.

It made it so hard not to reach out and touch his arm, brush his hair back from his forehead.

Bite him.

Just a little. Under his sharp jawline. Just to see what he would do.

She already knew they weren't going to talk about that kiss. She wouldn't let them. Everything was already too muddled.

And some things went away when you looked at them too directly.

He had once before. There was no reason he wouldn't again. Just as soon as he discovered what she was up to. Before even. She couldn't imagine him meeting her by the garden wall when The Duchess Games were over. Even if he didn't choose a wife.

"Did they upset you?" he asked, sharply, misreading her expression. Displeasure fairly sizzled off of him like steam from the kettle.

She shook her head. "No, just a bit of a startle, is all."

"Did they target your brother, do you think?"

She both smiled at the thought and felt every sharp edge of her spine rise like hackles. But she couldn't let Callum see her rage. It wasn't *ladylike.* "No, everyone knows he's far too good for that kind of thing. He's rotten at lying."

No, they'd come for her.

Hang ladylike.

She knew it was Juro, that arsewit, and she would make him pay dearly for it.

Starting now.

She stopped walking, tilted her head at Callum.

He narrowed his eyes. "What?" he asked. "The look on your face makes me glad you don't have a sword hidden on your person."

Oh, she did. It just wasn't the kind of weapon people expected.

"You were very kind back there."

He lifted an eyebrow. "And?"

She could lie to him, of course. But it felt wrong, as if every lie added together might crush her. If she could tell him the truth whenever possible, she might feel less itchy. He might remember, one day, that she only misled him when the stakes were high.

Or she was deluding herself.

Regardless, she could be mostly honest about this request. "Would you walk through the village with me?"

She worried at her lower lip. Perhaps she was asking too much. Why would the Duke of Tremaine take a stroll with Caitriona Sparrow, spinster and smuggler? Through Little Crumpet of all places?

"Is that all?" he asked, surprised.

"It might remind the other revenue men that you trust me."

Not to mention Juro and the other lads. They'd know she had connections. And the signet ring she had yet to steal.

Best of all, Juro would know he hadn't gotten to her.

"It's a bit political of me," she admitted.

"I'm in the House of Lords," he returned. "This is downright quaint when it comes to politics."

She wasn't entirely sure she liked being called quaint.

But then he held his arm out to her, like a proper gentleman escorting a lady through Hyde Park. "If we're going to do this," he said. "We do it properly."

She curled her hand at the crook of his elbow and tried not to read too much into the warmth and comfort that went through her at the contact. He made her feel both safe and desperately wicked. No one else had ever been able to do that.

They reached the village proper before she could make an utter cake of herself.

The villagers watched them as they passed, eyebrows raised, whispers passing back and forth. They'd be talking about this for weeks. Months. The day the duke walked through Little Crumpet with Cat on his arm.

"I suppose a kiss on the hand would be overdoing it?" Callum murmured.

"For Little Crumpet?" And from a duke? "Yes."

"Pity." She blinked at him. He didn't look her way, but his voice dropped. "Just as well, as that's not where I want to kiss you again."

Her head emptied. Just… emptied. No thoughts, no worries, no plans. Just a rush of want, heat racing up her thighs.

She cleared her throat. Twice.

She couldn't think of a thing to say that wasn't *please* and *now* and *again*.

She was almost grateful when Percival shattered the moment by trying to squeeze his enormous body between them. His tail wagged fiercely, like a whip. He jostled them both and then trotted away to be chased by three of the children. They hollered with laughter.

One of the merchants hurried out of his house to greet the

duke. The baker offered a basket of crumpets. When they reached the pub, Cat told Callum about the day Ambrose found Maggie asleep, fully naked, on the roof.

"I remember The Laughing Mermaid."

"You do?"

"Does Ambrose's brother still run it?"

She nodded. "He does, yes."

"I've never been so drunk as the night Ambrose fed me ale," Callum said, nearly smiling. He was different here, the line of his shoulders was less hard, his posture less exquisite. He looked human.

Granny Goodwin was the first to notice, sitting across the road on her stoop. Her shawl was the gray of a storm at twilight. "Well, aren't you a slice of cake?"

Cat couldn't help the startled laugh that burst from her. "Granny, did you just call a duke cake?"

"So I did," Granny chortled. The smoke from her pipe wreathed her head like pale flowers. "What's he going to do about it, eh?"

Callum turned and looked down his perfect nose for one silent moment.

Cat held her breath.

She needn't have worried. She knew him to be sharp and cutting, to be impatient with pretense, but never cruel. He appreciated forthrightness. That much hadn't changed. Would likely never change and she knew that now, having seen the people that flocked to him, full of demands and flattery and artifice. *That* Callum dismissed them with an icy flick of an eyebrow.

This Callum offered Granny a deeply elegant courtly bow. It was the kind that showed great respect for the recipient and was generally reserved for royalty.

And then he winked.

The stern, unyielding, exceedingly proper Duke of Tremaine *winked* at Granny Goodwin.

And Granny beamed like the sixteen-year-old girl she had once been.

Cat felt the invisible ribbons winding between her and Callum tighten. There was nothing she could do to stop it. While Cat tried not to hyperventilate at the feelings she refused to feel, one of Granny's crows landed on Callum's shoulder.

He went very still. "Is he a friend of yours?"

Granny cackled. "That's Humphrey," she said. "He likes you."

Humphrey hopped down Callum's arm to peck at the silver button on his cuff. "He likes shiny things. I think I am superfluous."

"That he does."

Callum raised an eyebrow at Cat. "Does everyone in Little Crumpet collect animals?"

"Taught her mother everything she knew," Granny interrupted proudly. "And she taught Cat. Cat's the best of us, I don't mind telling you. I like birds, her mother liked small, sweet creatures. But Cat will rescue anything. The meaner the better."

Callum smiled then, just a brief lopsided curve that she could not look away from. "I know." He noticed the oilskin tacked into the space left by a broken window behind her. "Did he do that?"

She laughed. "That's been like that for two years now. Bit nippy in the winter. Humphrey doesn't like that I covered it up. Thinks it's his own personal door."

Humphrey, hearing his name, cawed once for attention. And because Callum's button would not come loose. "Here, give him this," Granny handed Callum a bent and rusty nail. He accepted it as though he wasn't used to being given things dipped in gold. "It's not as nice, but it will keep him busy."

Instead, Callum reached down and yanked the silver button free from his sleeve. He did it as though it meant nothing. He did not even notice the involuntary gasp that came from Granny, from Cat, and from Old Pete pulling his cart up the road. Callum tossed the silver button in the air and Humphrey leapt up to snatch it, cawing with glee. He flew away to the nearest roof to admire his treasure.

"You'll never be rid of him now," Granny said.

Cat was very much afraid he would never be rid of her now either.

Trust Juro to try and steal every bit of sunshine.

He emerged from the pub, flanked by three of his lads. Strutting like he already owned the village, the smuggling operation, her connections. The small double-take he did when he spotted her there, unencumbered by custom agents, not on her way to Bodmin jail but instead strolling with the duke was sweeter than any of the champagne at Penhallow.

She wanted to cackle like Granny's crows.

Juro glared at her as he went on his way. Granny spat on the ground after him. Her crows jeered.

Cat left the village with a spring in her step.

Callum watched Juro for a long time. "Who's he?"

"A pain in the arse," she replied.

"I don't like how he looks at you."

She snorted. "He was being downright polite."

"Smuggler?"

She stopped. "What makes you say that?"

"He looks dodgy. Like a thief."

"How can you tell?"

"Cat, I know when a man stares at a woman and it makes the hairs on the back of my neck rise that he's not a good man."

"Fair enough," she said. "But it's not because he's a thief. He's just a git."

"I doubt he troubles himself overmuch with the law."

Cat watched him for a moment. "Come with me."

This was probably unwise. Actually, it was definitely unwise but she couldn't help herself. He had so much power as a duke, power he might well wield badly without even realizing it. As vindicating as it might be to let him scapegoat Juro, there were larger issues at stake.

She led him down the hill towards the beach, turning left.

The smell hit them almost immediately.

Callum stopped. "What the bloody hell."

"Welcome to the palace."

He only stared at her. She smiled a little. "The pilchard palace," she explained, motioning to the courtyard with gutters in the ground, buildings on three sides. "This is where we salt and press the fish. When we can." She caught Percival's collar when he tried to dart passed her. "I don't think so, boy-o. You're not going to meet a duchess after rolling in fish bones."

Instead of the boisterous industriousness of the entire village gathering to process the fish, the cellar was crowded with gulls and a heap of rotting fish bones. It was painful to see.

"The last shoal harvested was a few months ago. It's been a bad summer for them unfortunately. And on top of that, we couldn't afford enough salt to process the lot." She raised an eyebrow pointedly. "The taxes were too high."

"I was under the impression that salt for pilchard processing is not taxed."

"Sometimes. But everything else is taxed and where's the coin left with which to purchase supplies? And French salt is the best and we both know that's a problem."

"Might we continue this conversation elsewhere? That smell is... powerful."

They went back up the hill, away from the shouting gulls, the putrid fish.

"We salt and press the fish to eat, but also to squeeze out the oils. It's what lights your London lamps." She tilted her head. "Well, not *yours*, I imagine."

"I would remember the smell." He frowned. "Am I to gather you harbour some sympathy for the smugglers?"

"More than I do for the revenue men. You saw how they are, little men drunk on power. And we have to eat, don't we?"

"Don't let Armstrong hear you say that."

As if she would. "He doesn't care if we go hungry. He only

cares about the letter of the law."

"He's doing his duty to the Crown."

"Perhaps."

Callum rubbed at his neat beard pensively. "There's much talk about smuggling and illegal activity in Parliament. And the war. The taxes pay our defense against France. Who knows how long Napoleon will fight back?"

"Is that Armstrong's arguments I hear? Cornishmen are born and bred evil?"

"I'm a Cornishman," he returned, mildly offended. "And smuggling is a problem, you can't deny that. The law must be preserved. Especially now that we're at war."

"Those laws were made for you, by other people like you. They don't always help people like me. Never mind exporting goods, the taxes prevent us from salting fish and having something to eat come winter," she pointed out. "It takes a full bushel of salt to process enough fish to feed a single family over the winter. And it's already August. But I have no doubt you have made a great many speeches in Parliament."

The lift of his eyebrow was censorious. "I have."

"And do you think it's made a difference?" She shouldn't press the matter but the Callum she had known before was still there somewhere, under all that duke-ness. She wanted to chip away at that cold wall of privilege and power until she reached him. With her teeth, if need be.

He grimaced. "Not as much of a difference as I would like," he admitted. "The House of Lords is mostly just men shouting."

"Sounds tiresome."

"It's the way it is."

"How many houses do you own?" she asked. "Five? Six?"

"Twelve."

She forgot how to blink. "*Twelve* houses?"

"Twelve."

"That's too many." She was the one with the censorious eyebrows now.

"I suppose it is."

"But you probably have more of an effect as a duke with twelve houses than as another man shouting in Parliament."

"What makes you say that?"

"You must have a staff numbering in the hundreds. Tenants in the thousands."

"I suppose I do."

"And your actions affect them. Immediately, unlike I imagine a politician's work. If you lower the rents, mend broken windows, irrigate the fields. Pay your household servants a decent wage. Not grope the maids."

"I most certainly do *not*."

"I know. That's my point. Other aristos are not so decent, I assure you. Some maids flee in the night. Some villages run out of salt. These are things you can make a difference on."

"Legally."

"For you, yes. Not everyone is so lucky."

"That was quite a speech. Have you considered being a politician?"

"Bite your tongue."

He chuckled once and it brought her back to where they were, standing on a hill above the fish cellar, while she lectured a duke.

Well done, Cat. He kisses you and you show him a pile of dead fish.

Chapter Twenty

S HE WAS IN so much trouble.

Doomed.

Utterly.

Not only had Callum invited her unruly one-hundred-and-thirty-pound puppy to his fine manor house, but she had seen him smile. A real smile. Just like the one she remembered from when they were younger. At her table. And then again at Granny Goodwin with pilfering crows and pipe smoke.

She couldn't even allow herself to enjoy it.

Tell that to her heart, still racing in her chest. To her mouth, still tingling from his rough kisses. To her body craving more, so much more.

She could turn it into a game, one far more interesting than The Duchess Games. The Make Callum Smile in Public game. It might be as unlikely as turning herself into a duchess. But she didn't mind a challenge. Especially not a diverting one. There were several choices open to her: tease him, enrage him, mock him.

She *should* pretend none of this had ever happened, the incendiary moment in the closet, the primal chase, the burning kiss against the garden wall. It was safest.

She had no time for games.

And yet.

She was distracted from her inner turmoil by Lady Wandsworth. Just as well. Callum was looking at her out of the corner of his eye, as if he could read the worry and the need boiling in her belly. When they passed the drawing room, several murmurs rose at the sight of Percival, trotting at her side like a gangly pony.

Lady Wandsworth, who was very fine and had not spoken one word to her, came to the hall and sat right down on the floor in her beaded dress, opening her arms for an excited wolfhound who did *not* smell like rosewater perfume. He licked her face and she only laughed. "What a handsome prince you are."

Percival's tail whipped across Cat's legs in a frenzy of joy. Lady Wandsworth would not release him for a good ten minutes. Cat glanced at Callum. He glanced back at her, down his nose, cold and yet somehow searing. And there. Just there. That tiny twitch at the corner of his mouth again. Not quite a smile.

"Tremaine, what is the meaning of this?" His mother's voice was like broken glass, just waiting to cut. Cat saw the exact moment the almost-smile died, and she felt like baring her own teeth, and not in a friendly manner. The dowager did not even call her son by his given name, only his title.

"What is that…thing doing in my house?"

Callum turned his head. "And here I thought it was my house."

The dowager bristled.

"I've invited Miss Sparrow to bring her dog," he said coldly.

Cat smiled awkwardly. "Don't worry, Lady Tremaine. I won't allow him in the drawing rooms."

"I should hope *not*."

Really, it was like talking to an icicle. Where she could see how Callum's properness hid something else, how he appeared cold because she thought he was very much the opposite, it was impossible to read his mother. She could well be cold all the way through.

"I'll just take him upstairs," Cat said before she could say something else that would have the butler toss her out on her backside. She kept a firm grip on Percival just in case he thought to investigate Lady Tremaine to see if she might sneak him a custard tart the way Lady Wandsworth absolutely had. They bounded up the stairs, rattling the chandelier.

"Honestly, that girl," Lady Tremaine snapped. "I don't know what I was thinking."

"Mother."

Cat did not hear the rest of the conversation. She wasn't bothered by Lady Tremaine's opinion, and she certainly wasn't surprised by it. She didn't even disagree with it, really. She had no business in a duke's house. But Callum's response, his tone which would brook no argument, made a curl of warmth kindle inside her. And she could not afford that.

How many times did she have to remind herself of that?

Honestly, she was beginning to think she was becoming addled. Clearly rich food and champagne were not good for the mind.

Percival followed her into the sitting room she shared with her sister and then promptly proceeded to lose any ounce of dignity he'd gathered by his opulent surroundings. "Percival!" Viola cried out. Percival whipped his head around, spotted her on the settee and leapt, tongue lolling.

"Don't you dare climb on this furniture," Cat caught him by the collar. "This chair alone probably costs more than our entire cottage."

Viola bent down to hug him instead and he snuffled happily. Cat tilted her head. "You look better."

Viola grinned up at her. "I was better yesterday."

Cat frowned. "You were? You sneak! Why didn't you say?"

"I wanted you to have more time with the duke," she replied archly. "But now I'm back in the game."

Cat smiled weakly. She would *not* compete with her own sister for Callum. It was probably for the best. She had work to do yet. And Viola deserved every opportunity.

Viola rolled her eyes. "Not for the duke."

Cat tried not to wilt with relief. It wasn't as if there was a happily ever after waiting for her after she betrayed Callum.

"I know how he looks at you," Viola added. "And how you look at him."

She froze. "What?"

Viola kissed Percival's nose. "She thinks we're stupid."

"I do not!" Cat muttered. "And he doesn't look at me." But he did kiss her hard enough to ruin her for any other kiss until the day she died.

"Ha."

"Don't be absurd. Anyway, how would you know? You've been sniffling under the blankets."

"I have a window," Viola pointed out. "And eyeballs." She smiled smugly. "And gossip."

Cat groaned, dropping into a chair. "The gossip, I am quite certain, is about how ill-suited I am to everything in this house and nothing else."

"Not at all," a maid bustled out of Viola's room with an armful of bedsheets and a cheeky grin. Her brown curls were caught up under a little cap and her cheeks were rosy.

"Morgen!" Cat returned the grin. Morgen lived just down the street from them in Little Crumpet. Her mother brewed the best ale this side of Bristol. "What are you doing here?"

"Not all of us were lucky enough to win the duke's lottery," she said. Cat wrinkled her nose. Luck had nothing to do with it. Morgen laughed. "Never mind, I'd rather have the work for the next two weeks. You can't eat dancing and pianofortes." She rubbed Percival's haunches when he trotted over to her. "Hello, dog. Which one's this one again?"

"Percival."

"Is he the one that leapt into the cabbage cart and ate himself sick?"

Cat winced. "No, that was King Arthur."

"And that was three years ago!" Viola added loyally. "He's grown into his name. He's very regal now."

"If you say so."

Viola sniffed with pique worthy of the dowager duchess. Her pique did not last. It never did. "Cat, Morgen here tells me that Lady Siddal has been unceremoniously removed from the premises."

Cat sat up straighter. "She has?"

"Aye," Morgen said.

"Good. She kicked a turtle. She deserves it." Cat might not be as competitive as her sister, but she did have a rather well-developed sense of justice. Vengeance. Whichever.

"I don't know if that was the reason."

"Why else?"

Morgen exchanged a glance with Viola before replying. "Your dress was found stuffed under her bed."

Cat blinked. "Oh." Confusion warred with the glow of being seen, being thought of—possibly cared for. By Callum.

"So you see?" Viola crowed. "It's all going according to plan."

Cat snorted. "What plan? You had no plan."

"Maybe not, but I believe in fate and fate got us invited here." She narrowed her eyes with what could only be called unholy glee. "And I have a wager."

Cat raised her eyebrows. "You do? With whom?"

"Lady Ruby," Viola replied. She rubbed her hands together like something out of a gothic novel. "If I win, I get her cashmere shawl. I've never felt anything finer."

Cat did not ask her where in the fishing village she intended to wear such a fine shawl. "And what is her prize?"

"Nothing half so fine, I assure you."

"What's the wager?"

"The games, of course. I'm going to win them." She waved her hand nonchalantly. "But you can keep the duke."

Cat needed her sister if she was going to stay at Penhallow. The ladies would stop focusing on her if she was no longer competing. And she had every confidence Viola could win them over.

And in the meantime, she would find the signet ring.

She would steal it.

Again. Properly, this time.

And she would go home.

She would *not* obsess over the fact that Callum had stood against the revenue men on her behalf. Had kicked Lady Siddal, the daughter of an earl and the widow of a marquess, out of this house. And not just for attacking the poor turtle, but for stealing her dress?

Doomed.

Utterly.

Chapter Twenty-One

THERE WAS NOTHING like a spot of murder to pull one out of the doldrums.

The heat had finally broken, and it was a much more temperate day that brought the party out onto the lawns for archery. The sun was bright but inoffensive, even without the tents set up for the spectators. The footmen spent the better part of the morning setting out chairs, and tables laden with treat trays and towering displays of macarons and iced tea cakes. Strawberries floated in champagne, blackberries in lemonade. Everything sparkled, from the ladies to the sweets to the gentlemen.

Percival, having found Lady Wandsworth again, was in heaven. If heaven was made entirely of cookies snuck under the table and a saucer of milk. And it absolutely was. Viola rejoined the party to a warm welcome which allowed Cat to claim a seat in the furthest tent. She was just planning her escape when Summer dropped into the chair next to her, wearing a silk dress the color of peacock feathers. Emeralds gleamed in her dark hair. "At least this is better than watercolors," she said without preamble. "We were literally watching paint dry."

Cat laughed. "True."

"You are not participating?"

"My sister has recovered."

"Hmm."

Cat did not ask her what she meant by that. Here was another person she was going to betray, through no fault of their own. Summer would not take kindly to her brother being harmed in any way. Cat knew the potential for violent sibling defense when she saw it. She was well versed in it.

Summer poured tea from a small delicate pot painted with hedgehogs. "Here you go."

"Thank you."

Cat took a sip and choked.

Summer grinned. "I cannot be expected to survive this farce without proper fortification."

Fortification came in the form of double malt whisky. It burned a cheerful smoky path down Cat's throat, stealing all of the apologies she wished she could make, but could not.

"It's not French brandy, much as I'd like to serve some to that horrible Armstrong fellow," Summer said, adding more to Cat's cup. "But drink up. I need a partner in crime."

As this seemed a much easier type of crime than the one she was planning, Cat took another sip. "Your brother has always been very vocal in his support of Mr. Armstrong and his men."

"He has, I suppose. He likes it when things are clear."

The ladies lined up to have their turn at the bow. Helpful gentlemen hovered nearby, eager to lend assistance. Lady Ruby nearly stabbed one with an arrow when he attempted to adjust her stance without permission. Callum, wisely, was nowhere to be seen.

The archery butts were set up at the end of the freshly clipped lawns, against a swell of land and a copse. Cat felt sorry for any wayward rabbits. The birds had fled within moments of the house party trooping out in their finest riding habits and beaver crown hats.

Lord Kenilworth could not help himself and insisted on doing a demonstration. He missed the target entirely. When Blackpool drawled something in response which they could not quite make out, Summer leaned back in her chair. She sprawled mockingly, like any rakehell worth his salt. Her eyebrows raised tauntingly. "Go on then, Blackpool."

Ladies did not shout across the lawn. Twin sisters to a duke, apparently, did. Not being a lady herself, Cat snorted a laugh. The whisky might have had something to do with that.

Blackpool pushed away from the tree that he leaned against handsomely. A flutter of ladies in petal-hued dresses moved around him. He turned slowly, caught Summer's eye, and bowed mockingly. He really was an astonishingly beautiful man.

And he clearly had some experience with archery. He released three arrows in quick succession, hitting the target each time, all clustered at the edge of the main circle. He was good. Very good.

Viola was better.

"Well done!" Summer shouted, clapping enthusiastically. "Show him up, Miss Viola!"

Viola smiled, pretending that her skill was not entirely a thing of happenstance. Blackpool bowed again with a gracious smile. Viola blushed. Mr. Armstrong took the bow from Viola, hand lingering. Lady Ruby moved closer, eyes sharp.

"I want to set that man's smalls on fire," Summer muttered. "While he's still in them."

"Lord Blackpool?"

"Him too, a little," she admitted. "But I meant Mr. Armstrong. Parading about insulting the Cornish people while in Cornwall. Insufferable."

Cat drank to that. Deeply.

The dowager glared at her daughter, clearly displeased with her behavior. Summer sent her a saucy wave. "She only notices me when I'm being a nuisance," she confessed, reaching for a small cake decorated with candied orange slices. "But it's my revenge, you see."

"For what?" Cat asked. She was liking Summer more and more, and the dowager less and less.

"She named me Summer."

"Summer is a lovely name."

"I am Summer *Winter*," she pointed out. "Honestly, it was a call to battle from the start."

Cat snorted, clapped a hand over her mouth, and then snorted again. Summer, quite simply, howled.

And then Callum was there, emerging from the shadows of the house. "Are you foxed?" he asked, smiling that brief, gentle smile. The one that made her want to climb him like a ship's mast. She almost said so.

Oh dear. She was definitely foxed. Just a tiny bit.

"Certainly not," Summer sniffed. She listed slightly to the side. "Mostly not."

Callum pushed her back up with one fingertip. "All hands on deck," he said to his sister. "Have another teacake." His signet ring gleamed. Feelings she did not wish to acknowledge stirred under the whisky. The games were back on. The proper ones. The ones where she would lose everything by winning.

He raised an eyebrow at Cat. "And you, Miss Sparrow?"

"I'm fine," Cat replied. She tried not to giggle. Failed. She lowered her voice. "You're pretty."

He wasn't really, not like Blackpool. Instead, he was rugged and large, with that very unfashionable beard she longed to feel tickling the inside of her thighs. She lifted her cup and blinked. It was definitely empty.

"He looks like a fisherman when he comes to Cornwall and lets his facial hair grow in. Most unfashionable, you see," Summer said fondly, propping her chin on her hand. "It drives our mother to distraction. She firmly believes dukes ought to be carved from marble and be able to sweat gold."

Cat suddenly wanted to do battle against the dowager on behalf of both twins. She crammed a biscuit into her mouth. She was in no position to take on a duchess in her own house. Not while half foxed on whisky.

She stood up, hoping not to teeter and only half succeeding. She accidentally nudged Callum. "I beg your pardon."

"I look forward to it," he said, so softly she barely heard him.

"To what?" she breathed.

He ducked his head closer to hers. "You begging."

She went hot all over. *All* over.

The dowager snapped her fingers imperiously at her son.

Her son did not budge an inch.

The guests turned in their direction, expectant, curious. Their gazes sharpened when Cat stumbled back a step. Callum's hand at the small of her back prevented a complete retreat. She toasted them with her cup because she was just slightly too tipsy to stop herself. Summer snickered. "Good girl," Callum murmured.

Good Lord, the things this man did to her.

"Come, Tremaine," the dowager ordered. "You must present the winner with the red ribbon."

"Oh do, Your Grace," Lady Imogen sighed. Several of the other ladies agreed, if more hungrily. If they could have eaten his title like cake, they would have.

Summer snickered. Callum pinched her.

Cat fell a little bit more in love with him.

Horrified, she switched to tea. No more whisky. Ever.

Callum stalked towards the glittering group, scowling. Curtsies and bows erupted all around him. A footman in an old-fashioned horsehair wig jogged towards the targets to tally the count. Callum strode out to meet him on his return, escaping the clutches of social chatter. He nodded at the footmen and then turned, calling out without fuss or fanfare. "The winner is Miss Viola."

Viola's cheeks went pink. She exchanged a glittering, competitive glance with Lady Ruby.

"Will we never be rid of these Sparrows?" someone muttered loudly.

Summer stood, seething.

Cat also stood. Actually, she leapt to her feet. But for very different reasons.

It was Percival who alerted her.

He raised his head suddenly, whuffing softly, then growling. She'd never heard him growl before. His attention was focused entirely on the far corner of the garden, where the hedges gave way to a bit of wild. He knocked over his saucer of pilfered milk, every muscle tense. Later, she would give him an entire jug of milk and two kidney pies for his alertness.

He was the reason Callum did not drop to the grass, spurting blood from a hole in his chest.

She saw the rustle, the parting of leaves to reveal a pale glimpse of a face, a longbow.

"Callum!" Cat was running before she'd fully formed a plan. "Down!"

The expression of the others changed slowly, as if time altered. Surprise, disgust at her shouting, shock. She felt as if she was running through treacle.

She could not reach Callum quickly enough.

Not that she was able to fend off an arrow even if she could. It whistled and bit through the air.

Callum dropped.

Cat froze, choking. The blood in her very veins stopped. Everything stopped.

And the arrow slammed into the ground, inches from Callum's side.

He was safe.

Someone screamed. Lady Imogen fainted. Callum was already on his feet, striding towards the edge of the gardens, footmen coming from all directions, Blackpool at his side. His pale blue eyes speared her. "Get back," he ordered. "Percival, with me."

Percival loped towards him, nose twitching, eager to track.

"Who could do such a thing?" someone gasp.

"A child perhaps?" someone suggested. "I'm sure it was an accident."

Cat was equally sure it was not.

Chapter Twenty-Two

CALLUM AND BLACKPOOL returned from combing the grove with no culprit, just a few tracks that led into the fields and disappeared. No one seemed particularly concerned and the reigning theory that village children had snuck onto the grounds and stolen a bow to play with held.

But Cat wasn't so sure.

Killing a duke was as close to treason as you could get without involving the actual Crown. There would be no running or hiding for the culprit. You would need to be very careful and whoever had loosed that arrow was not careful.

Or else he had very bad aim.

Because it occurred to her that Callum had walked into the path of the arrow. She wasn't convinced it was meant for him. But had he not been there, had he stayed at the sidelines like a normal duke, drinking and being flattered, Mr. Armstrong would have been the target.

Had the archer known a bow from his backside, that was.

Killing a duke was not generally worth the hassle, but killing a Revenue Man?

Juro.

It had to be. No one else was so bold and impulsive.

Not to mention, idiotic.

If he took control of smuggling in Little Crumpet, half of the village would see the bowels of Bodmin jail. Or the noose.

She had half a mind to march down to the pub right now and strangle him.

A murdered customs agent on a duke's property, and a duke nearly killed in the process? They'd be overrun with agents and magistrates and soldiers already gathered to fight the French. They'd never make the drop. She needed a show of strength—better, a show of cleverness to get the others to stand down before Juro incited a riot. Didn't he understand this was meant to be stealthy work? Percival would make a better ringleader. And he had a tendency to chew on the furniture and occasionally piddle on the rug.

She waited until after dinner and after charades—which Callum did not attend to no one's surprise—until after late night billiards, until everyone had found their beds. She had last seen Callum striding across the back lawns under the stars in his haste to escape the party. She hadn't heard him return.

There was no better time.

No one heard her creep down the stairs, and no one saw her slip into his library.

There was only one problem.

The bloody signet ring was not on his desk.

Nor was it in any of the drawers, not behind a book on the shelf, not on the mantlepiece. She grew more and more agitated, cursing under her breath as she rifled through his personal belongings like a proper thief.

The ring simply was not here. Was he still wearing it? At this hour?

She slumped against the desk, dejected. But only for a moment. If she could process a pilchard harvest when it came in, stinking of oil and seaweed, then she could do this. If the signet ring was not here then it was most likely in his chambers. Perhaps he had taken it off and tossed it onto a table.

After all, no one would dare steal a duke's signet ring.

Enter Caitriona Sparrow.

Into said duke's bedchamber.

She darted inside, thanks to the key she had bribed into her possession. She didn't breathe until she saw the bed pristinely made, a single lamp burning on the windowsill. No Callum. The window was open, bringing in the sound of the wind, of crickets singing in the warm shadows. She could not allow herself to be distracted by the books piled here and there and her fingers itching to pick them up. Itching to know the titles, if he liked them. Were they histories? Farming manuals? Poetry?

She went straight for his shaving table with its serpentine drawers and lion's head pulls. There was very little frippery on the table, no cluttered scents or cravat pins. Just a comb and a jug of water for washing.

And his signet ring.

Relief and triumph went through her in equal measures. There was a curl of guilt, but she pushed it aside. She would not harm his name or his good standing. She closed her hand around the ring until it bit into her palm. *That's the badger*, as her Da would say. *And on with 'ee.*

"I admit the family coat of arms is not my favorite," Callum spoke suddenly from the doorway. "The acorns look like squashed tadpoles."

She jolted, biting down on a yelp. Callum leaned against the doorframe in his linen shirt and trousers, no coat and no cravat. He brought in the smell of the night: darkness, salt, green things. He wasn't smiling, his eyebrows drawn down. He watched her darkly, closely. Every part of her sparked alive, despite her situation.

"What are you doing here, Caitriona?" he asked softly. His voice was a pleasant rumble, commanding and deep.

She swallowed, trying not to look as guilty as she felt. There was no use lying. He'd seen the ring in her fist. Her brain raced, trying to find a way to salvage this. "I…"

He moved forward, graceful and predatory, kicking the door shut behind him. Her mouth went dry. He invaded her space, cornering her against the shaving stand. He gripped her chin lightly but firmly, tilting her face up to meet his gaze. "Tell the truth, Cat."

She bit her lower lip. His gaze dropped to her mouth, lifted again, flaring. He trailed his hand down her bare arm, soft as feathers. He forced her fingers open. "Why do you have my signet ring?"

She opened her mouth to lie, to tell him she had found it on the stairs and was only returning it. He'd never believe her.

A better lie then.

She sighed. "I was stealing it."

There was a beat of silence and then simply: "Why?"

She closed her eyes briefly because she couldn't stand the dark, gentle patience. Then she called herself twelve kinds of fool. She wasn't just a woman. She was a smuggler. She forced a smile, apologetic but also one that invited him into the joke. "I was dared to."

"Explain." It was an order, not unkind, not even angry. But there was something simmering behind the calm. She didn't blame him. And she didn't fully understand why he hadn't already thrown her clear off the property. Anything between them was surely not strong enough to withstand this kind of duplicity.

"You didn't think the Duchess Games were a completely public affair, did you?" she asked.

"Is that why my gardener found my ring in the bushes?"

"There are games within games. And there are ladies here who will do anything to catch themselves a duke."

"And you are one of them?"

She didn't answer.

"No, you never were, were you?" he said, mostly to himself. She was torn between asking him to elaborate and wanting to get out of this situation immediately.

"You should lock your bedroom door," she suggested. "We are not exactly above board."

"I can see that," he said. "And here I thought I had locked it."

"These games are more serious than you think."

"Are there rules?"

"Of course." It was difficult not to get lost in his gaze. He was dangerous, a current just waiting to drag her under.

"And what happens if you break them?" he asked silkily. "Surely, there's a punishment."

She swallowed. She was losing the upper hand. She felt it in the way her skin tingled and the muscles in her thighs went loose, her breasts heavy. She gave him back his ring. "I'll go. Right now."

He pressed closer. He gripped the table on either side of her hips. "I don't think so."

"Your Grace."

"We're not done here. I believe I asked you about your punishment."

"I don't blame you for calling the magistrate," she said, shakily because the wrong parts of her body were waking up. She was meant to be focused, careful. Not aroused. "But please, please don't. My family would suffer, and they haven't done anything wrong. They're not to blame." She'd never get the smuggling operation properly on its feet. What had made her think she could do this?

No. She *could* do this.

A right sight better than bloody Juro.

"I'm the one who stole from you. I'll…" she searched for an alternative to arrest. "I'll just go. You'll never have to see me again."

"Unacceptable."

"Please, Callum."

"Who knows what else you might have stolen?" He wondered. "A duke can't be too careful."

She blinked at him. His entire demeanour changed. The air was charged with something completely different. Her body understood it before her mind could fully catch up. Her nipples pebbled underneath her nightdress.

"I think a thorough search is in order." There was a glint of mischief in his blue eyes. It made her bud pulse hotly between her legs. "Don't you?"

"You're not angry?"

"On the contrary, I'm very angry," he corrected her. He eased back. She didn't like it. "Whatever happens here between us, Cat, it's not retribution. It's not duty or debt. Are we clear?"

She nodded.

"I'm going to need you to say it, Cat."

"I don't owe you anything."

"This isn't bribery or blackmail. Say it and mean it, Cat. Or go."

She should absolutely go.

"It isn't bribery or blackmail," she said instead.

He closed his fingers very gently around her throat, nudging her chin up with his thumb. "Did you steal anything else?"

"No." Her breath trembled.

"Show me."

Chapter Twenty-Three

T IME STOPPED.

Instead of blaming her, berating her, or shutting her out, Callum was creating a pocket outside of reality. Away from smuggling and stealing and etiquette. She didn't know how he managed it. How his cold gruffness evaporated at the very moment when he was most entitled to it.

Instead, there was only his searing gaze moving over her, his arms folding over his chest. His eyebrow lifting in command.

Show me.

His words echoed through her.

Her fingers touched the laces at the neck of her nightdress. She pulled them loose, slowly.

"Are you going to make me ask you again?"

She nearly whimpered just at the stroke of his voice, and he hadn't even touched her yet. "Maybe."

"Is that so?"

Another stroke, just from his voice, shivering over the back of her neck, down her throat. She swallowed and fisted the material of her nightdress, finally pulling it over her head. She was naked underneath, nothing between her and his hungry gaze. She faltered briefly, nightdress crumpled in a ball in front of her.

"Keep going, Caitriona."

She swallowed. "I'm not…"

"Not what?"

"I'm not like your soft aristos, Callum." She felt stupid just saying it out loud.

"No," he said, and she clutched her clothing closer. "You are lush and strong and perfect."

She met his eyes, startled. "I have freckles." Stretch marks. Scars from ropes and beach pebbles and puppy teeth. Rolls. Secrets.

"And I intend to lick every single one of them."

"Oh." It was all she could manage, a soft exhalation.

"Do you think this is the time to tease me, Caitriona?"

Her awkwardness melted under his approving perusal.

"Maybe," she said again, archly this time. Testing the border of his monumental self-control, daring him to lower the shield of his title. Just as she lowered the material and let it fall to the floor.

"Come here, Caitriona."

She took a step forward, paused. He growled.

She felt more powerful than a queen with a hundred armies at her beck and call.

He crooked his finger to draw her nearer and then circled it once. "Turn around for me."

She feigned innocence even as her breath trembled, and her nipples puckered. "Why?"

"Little thieves need to be searched," he said. "Thoroughly."

She turned on her heel, feeling giddy and lustful. Like she wanted to moan and laugh at the same time. She didn't hear him close the distance between them but suddenly his mouth was on the back of her neck. He dragged his teeth along her spine, beard tickling her skin until she shivered. He bit gently, just above the swell of her bottom. She jolted, sensation arrowing down the back of her thighs and into her very core. His fingertips dug into her hips, dimpling her skin. "Callum, please."

He bit again, then soothed the sting with his tongue. "You deserve a little punishment, don't you think?"

But he insisted on teasing her so she *couldn't* think. In the closet, by the garden wall. Here, finally alone in his bedroom. Thoughts of smuggled tea and revenue men fled entirely. There was nothing but his mouth, his beard tickling her, every part of her straining for more.

"I said, don't you think, Caitriona?"

And his dark voice, always his voice bringing her back to her body, the needs he aroused, inexorable as the tide.

"Are you punishing me, or yourself?" she asked pertly.

He stood slowly. "Good point."

And then she was suddenly on her back, sprawled over his wide soft bed. His fingers curled around her ankle, and he yanked her closer. "Better."

He leaned down and she reared up, wanting to meet his kiss halfway. He only smiled that dark, demanding smile and bent his head to her breast. He drew her nipple into his mouth with a long pull that made her gasp. His palm grazed her quim and she moved helplessly, trying to get closer. He was still fully dressed. The stark contrast to her nudity, to the way he eased her legs open, only made everything feel more intense.

He moved to her other breast even as he pushed a finger inside her, then another, working them as deep as they would go. The sensations stole every thought and worry right out of her brain.

"Do you know how long I've waited for this?" He groaned. "Take anything you want if it means I get to touch you."

He couldn't mean it.

But oh how she loved that he said it.

She clawed at his clothes, untucking his lawn shirt, threatening to rip it. He laughed, low and amused but when he removed it, his hands trembled. Just a little. Just enough.

He moved back up her body, gently rubbing his beard along the inside of her knee, up her thighs. His mouth ghosted over until she squirmed restlessly, and he laughed. "I think this is my favorite freckle," he said against the soft patch of skin above her mound. "It makes me wonder how you got it. Lounging naked in the sun like a mermaid." He licked it, as promised.

And then he licked lower.

She wasn't a spinster with secrets, a sister, a smuggler defending her territory.

She was the sweetest dessert. And she was being devoured.

Callum licked at her, groaning his pleasure. He nipped and lapped, using the flat of his tongue, the very tip. He pushed his fingers in and out, slowly, deeply, keeping a rhythm that threatened to drive her mad. And then he sucked her clitoris into his mouth, hot and desperate, rolling it gently, then deeply. Over and over again.

The coils of pleasure sharpened and tightened, tightened. Her release came in waves, cresting so suddenly that she arched, her back leaving the bed. She might have been embarrassed at the soft mewling sounds she made if she'd had the presence of mind to be. If they didn't so clearly and thoroughly drive Callum to distraction. If he wasn't so hard and hot against her, so smooth when she was finally able to take him into her hand.

"My turn," she said. "My turn."

She circled her fingers around his length, drawing them up and then back down. He twitched against her palm, groaning. "Cat."

She smiled at the raw need in the single syllable of her name. She commanded a gang of smugglers, several animals who would happily rend a man limb from limb but here and now was where she felt like a queen.

She worked him harder and then slid down the mattress to take him into her mouth. She licked up the side of him first, around the head. And then she glided down the length, swallowing him down as far as she could, hollowing her cheeks.

His hand fisted in her hair, tightened.

And then he jerked her up abruptly. She protested. She'd barely just started. She wanted him as weak with pleasure as she was. "No, siren," he said. "Too good. I can't spend before I get a chance to sink into those beautiful thighs, into that perfect pussy."

She ran her hands over his chest, the sculpted muscles of his arms, veins straining as he reined himself in. She bit his collarbone and the sound he made was thoroughly vindicating. "Hurry, Your Grace."

"You'll pay for that," he promised, and she fervently hoped so.

He dragged the tip of his cock between her lips, nudging against her swollen bud. He eased in, just a little, torturing them both. "So warm and wet," he said roughly in her ear, breathing ragged. "Let me in, Caitriona. For God's sake, let me in."

She lifted up to meet his thrust, pulling one knee up to widen the space between her hips, to welcome him, to steal the long hot moment and burn it into both of their memories. If she was a smuggler, stealing brandy and lace, then she could steal this for them. Just them.

He groaned, slamming into her. She lifted again and again, gasping, whimpering at the friction and the steady, ruthless pace he set. The weight of him was delicious, perfect. She felt another release building inside of her. She squeezed her intimate muscles around him as she came and he cursed, half-strangled half-awed, body straining. She followed, falling, spinning. Gasping.

Eventually she remembered how to breathe. He grinned at her, looking so much like the Callum she knew so long ago that she clenched around him. Her body didn't want to let go.

Her brain, that traitor, was already taking over.

He gripped her chin firmly. "Cat."

She blinked, looking at him.

"You're thinking too hard."

She smiled weakly.

"It can all wait until morning."

"You were nearly killed."

He shrugged, even as he disentangled himself from her. The air touched her sweaty skin. She shivered. "Hardly the first time," Callum said, bringing a cloth and the pitcher of water. "I went to Eton, remember?"

He ran the damp cloth up her thigh, and she moved to take over the task. It was somehow more intimate than the acts that had required the cleaning up. He stopped her with a sharp look of disapproval and continued to wash her, to run his strong hands over her until her muscles relaxed and her eyes drifted shut.

His voice again, soft this time, the perfect lullaby.

"Go to sleep, little thief."

Chapter Twenty-Four

STEALING FROM A bed at dawn was harder than it sounded. Harder than stealing lace and French brandy, apparently.

Cat woke to the solid warmth of Callum at her back, his breath soft on the nape of her neck. She felt sated and sore, exhausted and elated.

She felt too many things.

And she could not stay here.

The sky was pink beyond the window, the birds just starting their morning song. She could not be discovered here. A ruined reputation would make all of her plans so much harder to execute. She slipped one leg out from under the covers despite never having wanted to stay where she was more in her entire life. The other leg. One arm.

Nearly there.

She slid along the cool sheets. Her thighs ached pleasantly. A blush threatened to work up her neck at the memories of the night before.

Right. She was sneaking out.

Time to sneak.

One toe grazed the floorboards.

Callum snaked his arm around her waist and hauled her back against his hard body. "Where do you think you're going?" he growled into her disheveled hair.

She had to give her body a very stern lecture on this not being a good time to melt.

Or do any of the other things it very much wanted to do. Again. And again.

"The servants will be up soon," she said.

"Not for awhile yet. They don't disturb me until I ring for them."

"Oh." She swallowed. "Still."

He moved his lips over her neck, back and forth. His hand stayed locked around her, thumb grazing under her breast. She squirmed.

He growled in her ear. "If you keep doing that you'll not be going anywhere for a very long time."

Promise? She nearly asked.

His hold tightened as if she'd spoken out loud. She wriggled once. She couldn't help it.

"That does it," he growled in her ear. She was laughing even as he slid his hand between her legs, into the heat of her, already slick with need. The laugh turned to a moan. He cupped her breast, rolling her nipple between his knuckles and then urged her legs apart, his knee between hers until she was open to him. He pushed inside and she moaned again at the slow, thorough invasion. He moved, keeping a pace that made her want to weep, slow and deep all while circling her bud, until she bit his finger, drawing it into her mouth. He groaned, thrusting deeper, shifting the angle. Her blood heated and her release swelled, rippling across her thighs, crashing through her. She came with his name on her lips and he followed, panting harshly in her ear, smiling against her sweaty neck.

She turned towards him, still catching her breath. "You're smiling."

"Of course, I am," he said. "I'd be an idiot not to be smiling right now."

She traced his lips. "It suits you."

"Smiling is dangerous business."

She eased back against the pillow. "Is it?"

"If I so much as smile at the wrong woman at the wrong time, I might find myself betrothed by breakfast. If I smile at a gentleman then clearly I want to buy his finest horse. Or marry his sister. Or cover his gambling debts."

"That sounds…exhausting. Is that why you're so gruff?

"Gruff? Are you calling me bad tempered?"

She grinned. "Absolutely."

"Minx." His smile died. "When I first became the duke, I didn't know smiling might be my greatest weapon."

She dropped her fingers to his chest, tangling her fingers in his hair. There was something more, a story gnawing at him behind his stern eyebrows, his rare smiles. "Tell me."

"I was young," he said. "And stupid. For one, I left you behind here and didn't come back for years."

"I didn't expect any differently."

"That hardly makes it better. I wanted to marry you, Cat. I would have in an instant."

Warmth filled her, prickled with unease. She pushed it aside. Plenty of time for reality when she left this room. "I'm not duchess material, Callum. I'm the daughter of a fisherman."

"You're perfect."

She snorted a laugh. "Hardly."

"Perfect for me. And I fucked it up. All I can say is that grief does strange things to you, even stranger when the whole world gathers to treat you like a prince. I didn't realize how poisonous it all was until it was much too late. I'm glad I saved you from that, at the very least."

She frowned. "What happened?"

He shrugged one shoulder. "Nothing that hasn't happened to powerful men for centuries. I'm hardly special. But I didn't understand how much people wanted my power and my title. I wasn't a person anymore. Just a tool to be wielded."

She stifled a wince.

"Summer and Blackpool were the only people in my life who

cared, who demanded more from me. And you, of course. But I didn't deserve you."

"Now you're just talking rot."

"I didn't. I still don't. More to the point, you don't deserve what my world would do to you."

"I guarantee it would not be worse than pickling pilchard on a hot summer day."

He smiled again, a ghost of a smile. "My first year in London, I was feted and flattered until my head swelled. I made friends who I didn't realize were not friends at all. Some of them used my name as collateral in a gaming hell."

"That's remarkably rude." She was going to hell. Clearly.

"They would have lost their inheritances if I didn't pay their debts. And quite possibly the use of their legs. Gaming hells have enforcers."

"And you thought they were your friends."

"I told you, twenty-year-old boys are not smart at the best of times."

"That's hardly your fault."

"But I let it get to my head. I knew if I frowned at someone, they would get the cut direct. If I refused to dance with a debutante, she was done for, for the rest of the Season. If I left the theatre during an intermission, the rest of the Ton followed. It became a game."

"Ah."

"If I mentioned I liked someone's coat, their tailor doubled their business overnight. I once complained about someone's tea shop, just for the sake of being a little shit and the family lost their business within the week." He rubbed his beard. "Summer took me to their empty shop, and then by their tiny flat, where the father lived with his six children, all while delivering a blistering lecture."

"I can just imagine."

"She's always seen clearer than me. My mother was proud of me and Summer was furious."

"Your mother wants you to be a statue."

"The perfect duke."

"Same thing. So what did you do afterwards?"

"What do you mean? I vowed not to use my title for games, and I became utterly proficient in the proper disdainful distance, just as my mother had been drilling into me since I was a baby. More lessons, more speeches in Parliament."

She rubbed the spot over his heart. "And what did you do for that family?"

He didn't say anything. She lifted an eyebrow. She knew him better than that, however he might have lost his way then. He glanced away, embarrassed. "I got their shop back and I wrote a letter in the Times about how I only drank tea from their establishment."

"There's the Callum I know."

"They deserved more."

It was tempting to tell him the truth, but she knew what he thought about smugglers. He could forgive a little theft, but not that kind of dedication to law-breaking. Not her lying to his face, using his name for her own purposes, like so many others did. He'd doubt every word between them, every touch. And she could not have that.

"And that, siren, is why I am the Scowling Duke or Terrifying Tremaine, or whatever it is they are calling me this week in the papers."

"Terrifying Tremaine," she chuckled. "How very gothic of you. Should I be very frightened?"

He rubbed his beard over her throat, startling a giggle from her, then a moan.

"Very."

She grinned. "Promise?"

Chapter Twenty-Five

HIS DUCHESS WAS lying through her pretty little teeth.

He didn't know about what, only that something was swirling and boiling behind her nonchalant smiles. He might not choose a smile as his weapon, but he knew all about hiding behind an unyielding demeanour. She was distracted, worried.

He wanted to find every worry and decimate it.

She would never admit to worrying in the first place, never mind conveniently enumerate them for him. He'd removed Lady Siddal. He'd sent a proper bed and a thick new mattress to her cottage. He'd send his entire household to her cottage if it helped.

Better yet, he'd move her here. He wanted her in his bed, in his breakfast room, his library. Racing up the stairs with her pack of dogs. He would build the damn turtle his own indoor pool if she asked him.

"You cannot be serious, Tremaine," his mother snapped from the doorway.

He stifled a groan. He did not look away from the hawk nest. "I'm really not in the mood, Mother."

She sucked in a breath. "You will mind your manners and remember that you are a duke," she snapped.

"How could I forget?"

She exuded the chill of a winter morning. Cat thought his mother was trying to make him into a marble statue. She had already made of herself an ice sculpture. He was years passed tying to melt her defenses.

She sailed forward, slapping a piece of parchment on the table in front of him.

"What's this?" he asked, reluctantly turning around.

"This is a list of the suitable candidates for the future duchess in the order that appeals to me the most."

"I wish you all felicity on your betrothal."

"Don't be smart with me, boy." The lines around her mouth tightened with withering disdain. "And please do not tell me that you are harboring a tendre for that village girl."

"Careful, Mother."

"She is deeply unsuitable. Make her your mistress, if you must, but do not delude yourself."

Anger floored him, swift as the hawk Cat liked to watch outside his window. "That's enough."

"Don't be childish. I am only speaking the truth. I would never acknowledge her."

"That is no concern of mine."

"No one would acknowledge her, Tremaine. They would snicker behind their fans, make jokes at your expense. At the expense of the *title*. You'll ruin us all."

He pinched the bridge of his nose. "That seems dramatic."

"I thought you finally understood what it means to be the duke," she huffed with disgust before storming out. "Your father would be ashamed."

"You can go now, Mother," he said wearily. "Back to London if I am such a disappointment. I am not your creature. I'm a man grown, for God's sake. Enough. I will have kindness in this house."

"Be realistic."

He was sick to death of it.

"No."

The worst part was that his own mother was proving to him that he had been right to protect Cat from his world for all of those years. But surely he could protect her and be happy at the same time. She was the one who reminded him that he had so much power he could wield in better, more creative ways. He had let fear rule his every action for too long now.

They had thirteen wasted years between them. No more.

He crumpled up his mother's list and tossed it into the grate.

He felt immediately lighter.

"I heard every word," Summer announced, poking her head in. She was smiling from ear to ear, like a naughty child in the sweet's pantry. In fact, she held a small crystal bowl of marzipan birds in her hand. "Bravo, little brother. You deserve a sweet." She set the dish down with a flourish. "I nicked these from the tray of a passing footman. Pascoe, I think. The one with the red hair. Mother nearly made him cry. Again." She bit the head off a dove. "Have one. I am inclined to share since I have never heard you put Mother in her place quite like that."

"I hate marzipan," he pointed out.

"Good. More for me." She ate a canary. "I do like her, you know. I will enjoy having her as a sister-in-law."

"I haven't proposed."

She rolled her eyes. "Don't use the family heirlooms. They are hideous."

"Noted."

Chapter Twenty-Six

SINCE CAT COULD not get the image of the arrow nearly stabbing Callum in the chest, she walked down to the village. Percival accompanied her, tearing happily through the tall grass.

Cat marched like she was on her way to join the militia.

Fury built inside her, coal upon coal upon coal.

It paused, briefly, when she noticed Granny Goodwin's new window, glass shining like silver. She sat proudly underneath it, showing it to all who dared glance her way. Cat knew instantly that Callum had sent someone down to replace it. Quietly, without fanfare. Simply because it needed to be done.

And then she heard Juro's shout of laughter from inside the pub and the fury returned, lit from an internal fuse that would not die.

Juro might though. And at her hand.

She pushed inside the smoky pub with enough force that the clatter of cutlery and tankards died momentarily. Ambrose looked up from his stool behind the bar where he was wiping cups dry. He noticed her expression and set the cloth down with a sigh.

Cat found Juro immediately, posturing and bragging in the corner.

She skirted around the others, most of whom leapt out of her way. They did not usually see her fuming quite so ferociously unless an animal was involved, but they had long ago learned to get out of the way. Percival, sensing the change in the atmosphere, showed his teeth.

Juro sneered.

Cat punched him right in the face.

It helped her mood enormously.

Especially when he stumbled back, tripped on a chair, and went ass over tea kettle. Laughter swelled around them. Cat looked down at him, his fists clenched, his face red. "You utter arsewit," she spat. "You nearly murdered a duke."

Her duke.

Juro sat up, testing his sore jaw. "Told you she was too soft, lads."

"You tried to murder a revenue man, failed, nearly murdered a duke instead, and then failed at that too," she pointed out. "If you'd succeeded, what do you think would have happened, Juro? Do you think all of the customs agents would have fled, terrified of you? With the threat of the French army at our shores?"

He shoved to his feet. "You don't know anything."

"I'll tell you, then, shall I? Since you're too thick to work it out yourself. They would have called the magistrate, and then the army. On principle, they would have tripled the number of revenue men, because clearly we have something to hide. They would have sent in soldiers, because clearly we're ungovernable. They would watch the beaches, our homes. And then where would we be?"

The other men nodded to each other. Juro was more and more incensed. He spat blood from his split lip. "You bitch."

The men paused, waiting to see how she would react.

"Juro," Ambrose said.

Cat held up her hand to stop him. She appreciated the sentiment, but Juro's insults meant nothing to her. She didn't take her eyes off of him. "Are you trying to hurt my feelings? To make me lose my temper?" She yawned. "You should try harder because right now, you are very boring."

He went purple. She didn't stay to watch the explosion.

"Listen to him if you like," she told the others. "He'll lead you straight to Bodmin jail. Or the hangman's noose."

She marched straight back out, the door banging shut behind her.

Granny, peering in through the pub window, clapped.

VIOLENCE HELPED.

So did peeling potatoes.

Odd, but still true. There was too much energy coursing under her skin and nothing to do with it. She needed the signet ring, despite being caught. She needed a smuggling gang she could trust to help run her operation or it would flounder before it began.

She needed Callum.

Which was galling in the extreme.

So. Potatoes.

Truthfully, she didn't go looking for potatoes. She was pacing near the kitchen garden before going inside, waiting until she was sure she could smile politely without looking like Percival with a need to bite things.

As if she needed further proof that she would never be a lady.

"There's a face on you," Morgen said, stepping out from the kitchens. Her cheeks were pink, her hair curling around her face with perspiration. "Did someone abandon a puppy?"

Cat wrinkled her nose. "No. I'm cross, is all."

Morgen wiped her brow. "So's Cook. But I needed a breather."

"What's wrong?"

"Three of the maids have come down with sickness. Ate bad oysters though they were warned not to. How Londoners survive is beyond me. Who eats raw oysters on the beach when the shells are cracked open?"

Cat shuddered. "That's awful."

"With the ball looming and hundreds of pounds of vegetables

to deal with, it's beyond awful."

Cat thought of the afternoon of lawn bowling that awaited her. Of whispers behind fans, sugared violets. More champagne.

She might actually scream if she had to drink even one more sip of champagne.

"I can help," she offered.

Morgen raised her eyebrows. "Are you sure? You—" She cut herself off, grabbing Cat's arm and hauling her inside. "Never mind. We need the help."

"Percival, find Viola!" Cat tossed over her shoulder. "And don't chase the ball when the bowling starts!"

Percival lay on the flagstones under the rosemary and fell asleep instead. He wouldn't budge until she was done. Cat darted back out to kiss his furry head and then followed Morgen. The entire belowstairs was more crowded than the market at Padstow before Christmas. The air sweltered and the harried staff where shiny with sweat as they polished silver, transported baskets of linens, trays of tea and sweets.

The kitchen was even worse. Rows of maids stood at the tables while Cook bellowed orders like a drill sergeant. It was frantic, orderly, industrious. Familiar.

Cook barely glanced at her. "The kittens are fine."

"I'm glad to hear it, but I'm here to help."

Cook frowned. The maids exchanged glances. Abovestairs or below, Cat was always a little odd. She decided not to dwell on it. "That's kind of you but I don't have time to teach you."

"I can debone a haddock in under a minute."

Cook did not look convinced.

"It's true," Morgen said. "I've seen it. Her da was a fisher-man."

"Well, we've fish enough."

"You'll never get the smell off your hands," Morgen said. "You can't go to the ball stinking of fish."

"Those bloody toffs would never let us live it down," another maid muttered.

Cook snorted. "Can you peel potatoes?"

"I can."

"Excellent. Go on with ye."

She found the potatoes at a long table at the bottom of the stairs, not quite in the kitchen, just outside the housekeeper's room. Cat let the cacophony lull her, the murmur of voices, the shouts, the sounds of chopping and stirring and a cherubic-looking scullery maid singing a song to make a sailor blush. Cat remembered her mother singing it and her father scolding her, shocked and amused.

Cat scrubbed and peeled until her fingers wrinkled and her wrist ached.

It helped immensely.

Until…

"What on earth are you doing down here?" the dowager frowned at her. "I understand the natural order has been upset and I take responsibility for my part in it, but this is not helping. While you are a guest, you will comport yourself as a guest."

"She'll go where she pleases," Callum said sharply from the top of the stairwell.

His mother clicked her tongue. "And what are *you* doing down here?"

"What am I doing in my own house, do you mean?"

"You'll upset the servants," she insisted, shooing him like a fly. Cat bit the inside of her cheek to keep from chuckling at his expression.

Percival, sensing a game, raced down the hall on his spindly legs. He tossed his treasure at the dowager.

A soggy, half-chewed potato.

It hit the hem of her silk gown and landed on her delicate slipper.

The dowager yelped. It made her sound almost human. She clearly did not like it.

Cat was both mortified, and desperate to laugh. It bubbled in her throat, threateningly. She swallowed. "I'm so sorry, Your

Grace," she croaked.

The dowager kicked her foot out with the full displeasure of her aristocratic ancestors. The potato went flying. Percival barked his delight and chased after it.

Cat bit down on her lip very, very hard.

The look Callum shot her when he came back down a step, eyes widening, stern eyebrows lifting straight into his hair, did not help.

Not one bit.

Through the sheer force of her will, the giggle didn't escape until the dowager had huffed and marched back upstairs, calling for her lady's maid.

Cat dissolved into laughter, followed by a case of violent hiccups.

Morgen shook her head. "And I thought Little Crumpet was madness."

Chapter Twenty-Seven

MORNING PLEASURE AND laughing fits aside, Cat had work to do.

Callum might be able to force change through Parliament, but she could not. She had one avenue open her and she meant to take it. With both hands.

Whatever else it might say about her character.

About any chance of happiness with Callum.

She wasn't naïve. A duke would never marry her. But they could be a little bit happy, for a while, in secret. Until she ruined it.

At this very moment.

Here she was, back in Callum's library. The ring was right there on his desk. She couldn't very well steal it again. It would be far too obvious. But she still needed it.

She'd written several letters, vague but with the authority of a duke behind them they would do. More than do. They would get her people where they needed to go. Her cargo might make it to Bristol, Nottingham, London. Wherever it needed to go.

She risked lighting the candle to melt the red wax, sitting with it on the floor, under his desk. It was late enough that no one would come wandering by. She dropped the wax on the folded parchment—also stolen from his desk as any paper she might afford would clearly not be good enough quality for a duke. She pressed the seal in, waited a moment and then lifted the ring away. She did it several more times and then blew out the wick. She slipped the letters in the pocket of her dress, grateful for the out-of-date thickness of the fabric. Muslin would never hide it so well.

The dark quiet library was soothing, now that she had covered her tracks. It was Callum's space and it screamed his quiet competence, his power. Books lined the walls, a tray of crystal glasses and a decanter of whisky, piles of correspondence. She sat back on the windowsill, enjoying the quiet, watching the hawk fluff her feathers in her nest at the corner of the roof. Her thoughts were racing, details being organized in her brain, plans in case the first plans failed. But here, with the books and the wild birds and the smell of Callum's cologne, it might all just be manageable.

When the door creaked open slowly and Callum leaned in the doorway, part of her was not surprised. The man always seemed to know where she was. How to find her. How to draw her from the whirlpool of worry when it threatened to overwhelm her. She turned her head, smiling. "Hello, Your Grace."

"Little thief."

She would not wince at the endearment. He was playing a different game than she was. He was unfairly handsome, filling the room with his presence before he'd even stepped inside. Capable, strong, powerful. With that little half-smile he guarded like gold. She wanted to steal it away, as much as she wanted salt and brandy and contraband lace.

"What are you doing in here?" he asked.

She decided she would not lie, would not apologize. She leaned her temple against the cool glass. "I'm watching the hawk. Do you mind?"

"Not at all," he replied, closing the door behind him. The shadows enveloped them, comforting, touched by the light of the torches in the garden. "I'm sure we can find a better vantage point for your birdwatching."

"I like it here," she said simply.

"I like *you* here."

Another moment outside time, outside of their lives. Where consequences didn't loom on the horizon. Just Callum, just her.

She kissed him because he was so beautiful. Because she wanted to. *Had* to. Every moment together might be their last so she would seize them, devour them. His mouth met hers, the kiss turning deep and urgent practically before it had even begun. Her body knew the things he could do now, knew how he could make her feel and it wanted more. Wanted everything.

She wanted to fall into him. Wanted it desperately but her mind and her conscience would not be denied. They hovered, taking bites out of her pleasure. A kiss, a moan, a worry that he would never forgive her. Wouldn't understand.

"You're somewhere else," he murmured. He tsked like a disapproving professor. "Can't have that."

He yanked at the knot of his cravat, unravelling the length of cloth. His eyes never left hers, hungry, possessive.

"What are you doing?" she whispered.

"Helping you stay right here with me," he brushed his lips against her cheek, nuzzled into her ear. "Do you trust me?"

"Yes." She wouldn't ask if he trusted her. Couldn't.

He lifted the cloth and placed it over her eyes, tying it behind her head. The shadows between them turned to full darkness. She was suddenly very aware of her breaths, rasping and ragged in her own ears. The weight of her breasts, the throb between her legs. The hot anticipation racing through her.

She gasped when he swung her up into his arms, disorienting her and then anchoring her into his body at the same time. She suddenly felt free, safe, wild. There was no room for anything else, just Callum.

He laid her gently down on the settee, a cushion under her head. His fingers closed around one ankle, trailed up to her knee, inside her thigh. She shivered. She expected him to touch her heat, to slide his fingers over her quim but instead his mouth was on her breast. She started and his tongue dipped under her neckline, under the edge of her stays. Then he was squeezing her bottom, drawing her nipples out from behind their confines, hot breath in her ear. He was everywhere all at once.

It was intoxicating, exhilarating. Every inch of her skin was attuned to him, to the tickle of his beard, the press of his breeches on her bare knee, the stroke of his tongue into her mouth, again and again. She moaned and he chuckled, full of mischief and authority.

It fueled a fire she did not think could burn any brighter. Especially when he bunched her chemise up to her knees, so she was sprawled out, breasts bared, quim exposed. She felt wanton, wanted. Trembling with need.

He hovered, just out of reach.

"Callum."

"Look at you, spread out like my own personal feast." Every word touched her, stroked her when he did not.

She squirmed.

"You know what I want to hear, little thief." A faint whisper of a caress on her hip, a single lick over her nipple. "Beg me, Cat."

Her thighs pressed together. Heat pulsed. Her bud tightened, swelled.

"Callum, *please.*"

His mouth closed over her hot bud, startling a half-moan, half-shriek from her. He pushed two fingers inside her suddenly, deeply. She was already so wet they slid in, stretching, rubbing, sparking sensations that stole her breath. His tongue circled her, the tip dragging over her bud, dipping lower. He pumped his fingers at the same time, using his shoulder to widen her legs apart. She reached for him, his thick hair, the line of his arm, muscles working. *"Callum."*

She came with his name in her mouth, his fingers in her quim, his breath on her bud.

It raced through her over and over, too much, not enough, exactly right.

When it became too much she jolted, sensitive. He lifted his head, rubbing his beard on her inner thigh, tickling. She ran her fingertips over his jaw, dug them into his hair. "More," she whispered.

"Gladly." He bent his head, and she tightened her hold in his hair.

"It's my turn," she said. It was easier to demand, to give in to what she wanted when her eyes were closed. When she didn't have to wonder if she should be embarrassed. "I want you in my mouth."

He sucked in a breath and said her name like a curse. Or a prayer. "Cat."

"Now, Callum," she shimmied down the settee. "Do you want me to beg again?"

He muttered a filthy curse, one that had her smiling. She parted her lips expectantly. "Give me what I want, Your Grace."

The tip of his cock brushed her lower lip, both hard and soft. She reached up, closing her fingers around the base, squeezing gently. His breath went ragged. She licked the underside, up and down, teasing, with just a hint of teeth.

She wasn't the only one who would beg tonight.

He pushed between her lips and she welcomed him, sucking hard. She felt his hand slam down on the back of the settee. "Fuck, Cat."

This was the Callum she wanted for her very own. Not the duke with his perfect manners, his twelve houses, his gold buttons. Just this man, moaning her name, thrusting into her mouth, desperate but holding back. Eager but aware. Demanding but careful. Centering her just as she centered him.

She sucked harder, hollowing her cheeks, flicking her tongue. She raked her nails very lightly over his balls, then squeezed.

And then he was gone and she protested. Loudly.

Until he covered her with his body, pressing her into the cushions, thrusting into her wetness in one swift movement. She lifted her hips, meeting him stroke for stroke. They became one, sweaty and panting. Demanding. Answering.

He came with a hoarse strangled shout. She clung to him, smug with pleasure. The weight of him made her disappear, made her invisible and yet more seen than she had ever felt. Too soon, he shifted. "I'll crush you."

"I like it."

He kissed her softly, her lower lip, her cheek, a nip of her earlobe. Then he untied her blindfold gently, careful not to pull her hair. She blinked, waiting for the shadows to sharpen. His eyes gleamed, searching her face. "All right?"

She felt flushed and limp and downright cuddly. "More than all right."

He shifted so that he was on his back, and she sprawled over him, leg dangling over his. She rubbed her cheek over his chest, the hair a rough tickle.

"Cat." He said her name softly, as though she was a rare and precious thing. His big hand splayed across her back, warm and anchoring. "I love you."

She stilled, her heart pounding. She felt his in response, against the bare skin of her breasts.

"I've always loved you," he whispered. "I never stopped."

She knew she ought to pretend she was asleep, or make a jest, anything to lighten the moment. To shatter the sticky threads of hope and joy that threatened to tangle her up. But she had promised herself that in exchange for one lie, she would never otherwise lie to Callum.

And it wasn't as if she could ever become his duchess.

He was tensing slightly beneath her. She tightened her hold but did not lift her head from his chest. The letters were in her pocket, burning like vinegar in a cut. She ignored them. Just for now. Just for one more stolen moment. "I love you too."

He exhaled sharply. He gathered her closer. There was only the library, their hearts pounding together, his lips in her hair. "I should take you back to your room," he murmured. "To a proper bed."

"Before my dog chews your fine furniture."

"I don't care about that."

"I don't either."

"Not yet." She snuggled closer, logic and common sense be damned. "I don't want to be anywhere else."

Chapter Twenty-Eight

PENHALLOW WAS FULL to bursting with aristocrats.

And revenue men.

And nothing poked a pin into the bubble of a secret doomed romance like a revenue man.

The night of the ball finally arrived, and excitement thrummed through the halls. Cat found Viola in their shared sitting room, eyes shining. Piles of gowns glittered and sparkled around her. Green silks, delicate muslins, spangled ribbons. "Cat, you'll never guess," she said, clutching a champagne-hued gown to her chest. "Lady Summer sent dresses for us to wear."

"That was very kind of her."

"I think you should wear this magenta one. The color would suit you."

Cat smiled gently. "Vi, these dresses are for you."

She frowned. "Don't be silly. Her lady's maid specifically said it was for the Sparrow *sisters.*"

"Any dress that fits you and Lady Summer is not going to fit me," Cat pointed. "I'm too… everything."

Viola frowned harder. "But your dress…"

"Will have to do," Cat said, refusing to wonder what it might be like to wear such a vibrant dress with so much embroidery. Tonight, she would wear Matthew's trousers under her ten-years-out-of-fashion and not-quite-formal-enough dress. It had been a gift to their mother from the captain, a redingote with a boned stomacher and scoops of lace she had sewn on just this morning. She needed to be remembered, but not noticed and it would do the trick. Should someone later investigate a haul of contraband on the night of the Tremaine ball, more than one person would recall her dress having remarked their grandmother had one just like it.

Every detail had to be perfect. Every part of the plan needed backup.

Not to mention that muslin dresses did not hold up to running or hauling or sea spray.

"I think you should wear the green," Cat told her sister. "It will be brilliant with your eyes."

Those green eyes which watched her shrewdly. "Is everything set for tonight?"

"I don't know what you mean."

She sniffed. "I know you're trying to keep me out of it, but I can at least keep the custom agents distracted."

Cat hugged her. "I appreciate it, but I want you to enjoy yourself. When are we likely to be invited to a ball again?"

"Between the turtles and the dog and the spoons, not likely." She grinned. "Do you think I'll open the ball on your duke's arm? The dowager hasn't announced the winner yet. Ruby is positive it will be you though."

Cat snorted. "Definitely not. Percival dropped a chewed-up potato on the dowager's foot."

She'd sent Percival home to Matthew as a precaution. He would chew something prohibitively expensive if he was left unattended. Or Lady Wandsworth might steal him from the room. From Cornwall altogether.

"Good point." Viola reached for the green gown. It had tiny gold leaves along the daring neckline. "Will you help me get dressed?"

Cat helped her sister into her stays and her dress, lacing up the ribbons at the back. She wore her tiny pearl around her neck.

"You look beautiful. But it needs something."

She glanced around, settling on a decorative gold cord sewn onto a cushion. She unstitched it while Viola gaped at her. "You won't even let Percival *look* at the cushions in here."

This was her last night at Penhallow. What was the harm?

She wound the gold through Viola's hair. The candlelight caught it, gleaming. Viola grinned at her reflection in the cheval glass. "It's worth the risk of arrest."

Cat grinned back, feeling lighter. This was why she was risking arrest, not for hair baubles or silk. But for that happy, carefree expression on her sister's face. It was worth it. For one night, Viola wouldn't have to worry about the next meal and her brother would not have to go out in the boats anymore, fighting storms and the French navy. After a couple more drops, she might even be able to get him that apprenticeship with the blacksmith.

She put on the blue dress, pants well hidden under the wide skirts. There was a small split bum-roll that tied around her waist, creating a silhouette that hid the extra material underneath. Best of all, the skirt was a separate piece that could easily be removed. She'd already hidden proper boots at the edge of the garden.

She was ready.

The neckline was square instead of the more popular rounded lines, and her cleavage was… noticeable. She'd forgotten how the old styles pushed the breasts out.

"I take it back," Viola said. "You don't need a new dress. That looks perfect."

Cat wrinkled her nose. "I look like the lusty tavern wench in a bad gothic novel."

"You look like a goddess."

"So do you."

"A fairy princess, maybe. But I'll get there."

They descended the stairs together, candles burning in every sconce and lamps on every table. "The Sparrow sisters at a ball," Viola breathed as the music drifted towards them. "Who would have ever guessed?"

"And I don't even have a badger or an injured gull in my pocket," Cat laughed.

"The night is young," Viola shot back drily.

"Make sure you eat the roasted potatoes," she added. "I spent two hours peeling them."

The ballroom was something out of a storybook. Marble statues lined the walls, draped with roses. Half of the greenhouse had been moved inside, to create little jungles of privacy in the corners, potted trees dripping with oranges and lemons and flowers she had never seen before. Hundreds of beeswax candles burned in crystal chandeliers overhead. Every accent and chair and ribbon that was not a pristine snow-white, glittered gold. Even the musicians wore gold cravats and gold gloves, and the effect was stunning. Excessive.

"What an... interesting dress."

Cat curtsied, smiling as though the dowager's tone wasn't caustic enough to peel the very expensive wallpaper from the walls. Viola curtsied beautifully, successfully drawing the dowager's attention away from her.

Summer stepped out of the receiving line, breaking protocol. "That color is lovely on you, Miss Sparrow."

Cat curtsied again. Lady Summer leaned forward slightly. "I'll send whisky."

Cat grinned.

Callum was next to be greeted and his eyes flared when she paused in front of him. She suddenly *felt* like a goddess.

There was no time for talk as the line of guests pushed behind them. Cat took a turn about the room, making sure to be seen by Mr. Armstrong. Viola found Ruby and they drew back to whisper, heads bent together.

There was no better time.

It was easy to get lost in the crush of people, to let herself be carried to the glass doors already opened to let in the night air. The dowager no doubt disapproved, but the bodies would litter the dancefloor before midnight if fresh air didn't circulate. Fainting would be unavoidable.

She hurried between the hedges, snuck out past the flagstone border and retrieved her boots from under a bush. She removed her overskirt and her padded roll, hiding them under the leaves. Matthew's trousers and the removal of her dancing slippers allowed her to run home down the path. The moon was a sliver, barely offering light.

She clambered down the slipway, the waves crashing gently below. There was no storm on the horizon, no customs agents on her heels, no bright moonlight to give away the boat.

One problem.

There was also no gang of smugglers waiting for her orders.

The beach was deserted.

Bollocks.

Captain Davignon's ship lurked in the shadows. This was the time. But she had no lander to bring him in, no slipboats, no tubmen to carry the goods.

No one.

She was alone on the beach with her lantern and her secret codes.

Confusion, frustration, anger boiled in her belly. Her hands shook with the force of it. This was her chance. Possibly her *last* chance.

She lit her lantern, trying to calm her pulse. She covered the flame, and uncovered it, the pattern asking for a ten-minute pause. *Just ten minutes. Please.*

She sagged with relief when the answer came. He would wait. But she knew if he was spotted there would be two options: he would leave and take her last chance with him or he would dump the cargo and she would have to fight the water and Juro's men to claim it.

Because there was no doubt whatsoever in her mind that Juro was behind this particular little development.

And planting him a facer was unlikely to help this time. Even if it would make her feel enormously better. Enormously.

She raced back up the slipway and down the road to the village. The windows were yellow with candlelight, the air fresh with salt and the laughter of families sitting outside. The pub fairly rocked with noise. She slipped inside, with her cleavage and her curled hair and her brother's trousers.

Ambrose was the first to see her. He shook his head, sympathetically. She knew he'd have been there to help but the slipway and the beach were nearly impossible with his bad leg.

Juro was the second to spot her. He was set up on a chair like a throne, waiting. The village men glanced between them both, most not able to meet her eyes. Only his best mates grinned at her smugly, just as he did. "Cat. Bit overdressed, aren't you?"

"What the hell, Juro?"

"Is there a problem?"

"We agreed tonight was the night."

He took a swig of ale, smirking. "Did we?"

"The ship is waiting," she ground out. "What game are you playing?"

"See, we have the numbers and the muscle. This operation should be ours."

"It was my idea, arsewit."

"But you need us."

"And you need my beach, my code, my connections." She pulled one of the letters from inside her bodice, flashing the red wax seal with the crest of the Duke of Tremaine. She only felt slightly sick doing it.

Juro narrowed his eyes. There was a murmur around us. "Hand it all over and we'll make sure it runs smoothly."

She laughed. It was sharp, a bullet of a sound.

"Then unload it without us." He flourished his hand. "Go on."

They had her over a barrel. And they knew it.

They would wait until the ship dumped the barrels and casks and they would steal it from her. She wouldn't be able to stop them. Anyone could walk into the sea and claim a bounty. Wrecker's law.

She wanted to scream.

She spun on her heel and left, their laughter snaking behind her, pinching at her. Muttering, she stopped on the stoop, searching for a suitable weapon.

Do it without us.

She couldn't do this alone. It was utterly impossible.

She thought of the women forming lines in the cold water to bring in the pilchards. Of the maids in the duke's kitchen working together to feed hundreds of people. Chopping, boiling, peeling. Serving, cleaning, scrubbing.

Together.

Cat rammed the pole into the handle of the pub's door, locking it tightly against the frame.

She turned on her heel.

"Granny, I need your help."

Chapter Twenty-Nine

PENHALLOW MIGHT BE full of aristocrats.

But Little Crumpet was full of fishermen and miners and farmers.

Better yet, it was full of wives and daughters and mothers and spinsters. Full of women.

When Cat made it back to her beach, she wasn't alone. Margie, the baker's wife with arms twice the size of his was with her. Lowenna, Morgen's mother, Demelza with her sisters. Granny and her crows. And countless others with their baskets and sacks and wheelbarrows.

It was unorthodox, just this side of mad. It would never work.

It was perfect.

And that's why it worked so well.

When she first saw the faint outline of the ship against the sky, sailing away, dismay and disappointment filled her. She might have wilted with it were it not for the other women.

Captain Davignon was sailing away, and she could not blame him. If the revenue men caught him they would claim his cargo and saw his boat in three. If the French found him, he was done for. If the British Navy spotted him, it would be worse yet.

But he was made of sterner stuff and had always treated her mother well.

He dumped the cargo overboard before leaving, giving her

one last chance. Without the women of the village at her back, she'd never bring it to shore. In minutes Juro and his men would come charging down the slipway to steal it all.

Not in this lifetime or any other.

Margie was the first to reach the barrels, bobbing like corks. Cat charged in after her, the cold water soaking into her pants, pulling at her bare feet, whipping pebbles against her ankles. They dragged it to shore, panting for breath.

Together they swam out, pushed the barrels and casks closer to the beach, pushed and pulled to get them on the shore. Arms cramped with exertion, lungs burned. Lowenna went under, shoved by a barrel caught in a wave. Demelza pulled her back up.

She'd never pushed so hard in her life. Nor been in equal danger of drowning.

She loved every moment of it.

The promise of self-sufficiency, of comfort. Vindication.

And then Matthew was there, taking the heaviest barrel before it could sink her. She spat out sea water. "Let me carry this. I'm not useless, you know," he said.

"I never thought you were!"

"I can do this. But you can do the rest. The dreaming and the planning."

"And the bossing."

"That too."

She let him take the weight of it, and then took the weight of the next one, Margie at her side. By the end they were drenched and sweaty and smiling from ear to ear. A heap of barrels and two casks sat on the pebbles, full of promise.

The next part was even trickier.

Hiding the contraband was of utmost importance. Without the water to aid them, without tubmen to carry the barrels over dry land, they had to get creative. The casks went into the caves. She'd let Ambrose and his brother have first crack at the brandy. There wasn't much and it would need to be let down some to be drinkable.

The rest of it, the oilskin-wrapped tea, the fine lace, it would need to be moved immediately. Some of it would fit in the cellar under the cottage, but it would be the height of reckless to hide it all in one spot, especially with Juro on her heels. Lowenna had a cellar and Margie's sister-in-law had married a merchant with a fine house with a priest's hole still accessible under the stairs. Demelza had trunks full of old dresses that had belonged to her grandmother. Lace would lay nicely between them until Cat arranged for suitable transportation.

They had baskets filled with lace, jars of tea, bottles of over-proof brandy from the casket that was leaking. They raced through Little Crumpet, Matthew keeping an eye out for revenue men not currently dancing under the chandeliers of Penhallow. If they were about, they did not stop them. Women bustling by with baskets weren't even noticeable.

Cat would have danced a jig if she wasn't so tired.

Bone-tired.

Loving it.

There was enough profit to be had to buy food, even some luxuries. Every woman who had helped her, Granny included as she had sent out the word to the women, would receive a cut. If Juro's lads came back they would get five guineas, same as any muscle. But they'd wasted their chance at a proper cut. Juro would get nothing at all.

When she got back to the pub, the door was open. Granny sat with her pipe, grinning. "Ambrose kept them inside as long as he could. He threatened to ban them from the pub forever if they broke his windows. And then he claimed the back door was stuck and wouldn't let them by."

Ambrose would also get a cut.

"You look smug as three cats in a creamery," Granny said. "It suits you."

Cat's arms were like jelly. "It does."

"Best get back to the big house before Juro makes trouble."

"I can handle him."

"Aye, you can." Humphrey cawed once from the roof, fluffing his feathers. "On with thee."

Cat's journey back to Penhallow was considerably slower than her journey out had been. Everything hurt. She kicked off her boots, exchanging them for the dancing slippers. Off came the pants, back on went the bumroll and the skirt. She was no doubt flushed and her hair a bit wild, but at least it was mostly dry. Hopefully no one would notice after several hours of drinking champagne and by candlelight. She'd pretend she had danced too exuberantly in the heat of the ballroom.

It was the best night of her life.

And the worst.

Chapter Thirty

THE CONTRADICTION TO the bruising work of dragging barrels out of the sea and the glittering waves of exquisitely dressed aristocrats was a jolt.

The wild press of energy, the laughter, the scorn, it all swirled with the exhilaration and the exhaustion she already felt. She was calculating profit margins as she glided between dancers, seeking out the refreshment table. She might actually kill for a cup of lemonade.

"You see, Mr. Armstrong," Viola said with forced cheer behind her. "I knew she would be here somewhere."

Cat stilled then turned, pasting on a cheerfully curious smile. "Were you looking for me?"

"Where are you been? You look dishevelled."

"Mr. Armstrong," Viola said. "That is not very gentlemanly."

"But no doubt true," Cat said. "I was dancing. It's very warm in here."

Mr. Armstrong, sweating into his cravat, could not argue.

"All the same," she added. "I thank you for the reminder. I'll have my sister help put me to rights. If you'll excuse us?"

"Just one moment, if you please."

The music swelled around them. Someone laughed too loudly. Beeswax and perfume clogged the air. Cat felt it all like nails along her spine. Why was he singling her out? Watching her?

What did he know? "Yes?"

"I have questions."

"Certainly. How may I help?" She moved towards one of the collections of lemon trees. The fewer people who could overhear, the better. There was a spill of wine on the floor.

"I received an anonymous tip that there was smuggling activity occurring tonight."

"How dreadful." She set her cup down. "But what does that have to do with me?"

"Your name was mentioned."

She laughed brightly. Behind Mr. Armstrong, Viola was trying not to appear as though she wished to stab him in the kidney with a shrimp fork. "Surely not."

"It does seem unlikely," he admitted, clearly not convinced. But also just as clearly eager to make a dramatic arrest.

"After all, you were the one who said women were too dainty for crime," she pointed out.

"All the same, you come from the village, surely you know something."

"I'm afraid I don't. I've been here all week, same as you."

"You say you were dancing, but I did not see you."

"I don't see how you would have," she murmured, forcing herself to sound calm. To sound confused, like a spinster from a fishing village out of her element. "It's quite the crush."

"Who was your partner?"

Bollocks.

"Lord Blackpool," she blurted out because he seemed amiable enough and mischievous enough to play along if he was questioned. And it seemed unlikely Mr. Armstrong would dare question an earl, especially a friend of the duke. He preferred to exert his power over the little fish in his little pond.

"And yet there's sand on your hem."

She glanced down. "So there is."

"Why is that, then, Miss Sparrow?" His question was suspicious, bordering on gleeful. And loud. He wanted an audience.

Someone to blame.

"I live in a fishing village," Cat pointed out. "There is always sand on my person."

Viola rolled her eyes and fluttered her lashes behind his shoulder, looking like a confused goose. When Cat just stared at her, Viola mouthed a curse, and then pressed the back of her hand to her brow, fluttering her eyelashes again. Oh. She wanted Cat to swoon.

"Miss Sparrow, you will answer me, in the name of the King."

She fluttered her eyelashes.

"There you are," Callum said smoothly before she could drop to the floor. She heard the stone in his voice, even as he kept his every movement painfully polite. Cat curtsied, her skin prickling a warning.

"Your Grace," Mr. Armstrong greeted him effusively. "I was about to send for you."

"You were going to *send* for me, Mr. Armstrong?"

He gulped at the icy rebuke. No one but the royal family *sent* for a duke.

"Beg pardon," Mr. Armstrong said. He reddened but he did not back down.

Double bollocks.

"I received distressing news about the lady. And illegal smuggling activity."

Callum raised an eyebrow. "Don't be absurd."

"She knows something, Your Grace. She lives in the village."

"The village borders my estate, Armstrong. Tread carefully."

"Of course, of course! I only meant that she might be of help to my investigation."

"She might," Callum said. "But not tonight. I have come to claim our second dance," he held out his hand. It was a courteous command but a command, nonetheless. Cat couldn't have said why it sent ice through her.

Cat didn't know if Armstrong would have pushed further, or even if he truly believed she had some kind of information. But he was no match for the Winter twins.

"Mr. Armstrong," Summer interrupted smoothly. She wore a stunning gown patterned all over with red pomegranates and green leaves. Emeralds shone around her throat and wound through her hair. "We are in need of a fourth for a game of whist in the card room. Say you'll join us?"

Mr. Armstrong did what any sane man would do when faced with a request from a duke's beautiful sister. He stammered and bowed. "O-of course, your ladyship."

Summer led him away. Cat's shoulders relaxed slightly.

Not for long.

"Miss Sparrow."

Cat took Callum's arm because what else was she to do. No amount of premonition could change this. He did not lead her to the dancefloor but instead out of the ballroom altogether and into his library. Not his library. She'd give anything not to have those memories tainted.

A single candle burned on his desk. He wore his signet ring. And anger in his eyes.

"Callum."

"Miss Sparrow."

He advanced. She swallowed, stumbling back a step. She saw the walls rising up all around him, all stone and duty, but there was fire there too. And it wasn't the kind that warmed you on a cold night. Still when he leaned closer, she tilted her head back. His mouth hovered, just above hers. He rubbed his thumb along the neckline of her gown, her exposed cleavage, dipped lower. She caught her breath, every nerve sparkling in anticipation. He grazed her nipple, exhaled.

And pulled out the letter sealed with his crest from inside her stays.

"Care to explain this?"

Chapter Thirty-One

S HE HAD ALWAYS known this moment would come.

Of course, she had.

She assumed she would feel regret, sorrow, shame.

And she did. But the panic was a surprise. It welled in her chest, more fear and anxiety than a hundred revenue men might cause. "Callum."

"You lied to me."

She couldn't argue. But she might make him understand. If she was very, very lucky. If he was willing to listen.

He did not look particularly willing to listen.

There was menace to his cold anger, to the taut lines of his body, the betrayal in his pale eyes, pinning her. It wasn't the power of a duke, but the simmering force of a man betrayed.

"You played me for a fool, Madam."

"I didn't," she insisted. "It wasn't like that."

"You don't deny you used my seal?"

"No."

He barked a laugh, but it was cold, harsh. "There's that at least."

She wanted to give the letter back. Give them all back. But she couldn't. The women who had risked everything for her and would continue to risk everything deserved to know that she could protect them.

"I did it for the village. I haven't used it. And it's nothing that would malign you in any way."

The disdain was clear in the angle of his glare, the set of his jaw. She was watching him turn back into a marble statue.

"What would you do if your sister was hungry? Both my siblings need me."

"Like a fool, I admired you." He ran his hand through his hair. It fell right back into tousled lines. The hair of a duke, not a mere mortal. "All these years, I thought you made me a better person."

"I—"

"But you're just like all the others, aren't you? Playacting for a duke."

She flinched. She knew how that would cut him.

"It wasn't like that." She had to make him understand that much at least. Nothing that had passed between them was part of this. It had nothing to do with smuggling or contraband or stolen rings. But she had always known, deep down, that he wasn't for her. That she could not be a smuggler and a duchess. Never a duchess. But she couldn't let him think he meant nothing. Not when he meant everything. "Callum, I lov–"

His voice was the cold lash of rain at the windowpane.

"Don't."

"But–"

"No." She'd never heard anything more final. It was ice closing over a pond. She saw it in the blue of his eyes, going cold and gray. "When you said those words to me in the library that night," he continued putting the pieces of the puzzle together. "Those letters were in your dress, weren't they?"

She nodded mutely.

"You played me well, that much I'll give you."

"Callum, it wasn't like that. You have to—"

Summer appeared at the door. "There you are. Mother wants you to close the dancing seeing as you did not lead the opening as she promised. If you don't choose, she will."

"It doesn't matter anymore." He held Cat's gaze before stalking out of the library.

Summer frowned at his back, then at Cat. Cat smiled, pretending her eyes weren't welling with tears.

"Take heart, Miss Sparrow," Summer said. "I don't know what just happened, but my brother is a good man. The duke, on the other hand, is frequently an ass."

Chapter Thirty-Two

C AT WENT HOME.

What else was there to do? To say? What was the point in staying to torture herself, to watch Callum dance with a perfectly trained aristocratic lady, all smiles and diamonds? To see them curtsy and bow until his transformation into a marble statue was complete.

The village women had risked their lives for her and her schemes. She could not stay here and mope. She owed them so much more than that.

As it happened, it turned out she was perfectly capable of moping and working at the same time. She walked all the way home in her pretty gown, leaving the rest of her belongings and a note for Viola. The sea welcomed her and the tiny cottage with yellow lamplight at the windows. Her dogs pressed against her, tails wagging.

Her brother took one look at her and asked no questions. He passed her his mug of ale.

She did not sleep. Her old lumpy mattress had been replaced with a feather tick and a beautifully carved four poster bed. Callum had sent it without telling her. Matthew had performed some interesting maneuvers to keep the trapdoor hidden while the bed was carried inside by three footmen.

She sat up making calculations, working out transport routes, wondering where she could hire a barrel maker, how best to hide packets of tea, choosing the next cargo: more lace, green tea, salt.

She could not be a duchess. Or a mistress.

But she could be this. She could do *this*.

Even through a chest that felt so tight it might crack. She could survive anything if it meant keeping her sister and brother safe and healthy, if it meant extra potatoes for Granny Goodwin come winter, salt for the next pilchard harvest, pain cream for Ambrose's leg. Callum would return to London and her life would go back to being her own.

She briefly wondered how it was possible to feel both unbearable numbness and unbearable pain.

But wondering did not pay for salt. It did not mark the tides or track the revenue men. It did not fight the French.

Viola came home the next afternoon. She wasted no time in harassing her. She was much braver than Matthew. "What happened?"

"It doesn't matter now."

"I can see by your face that it does. And by the way the duke was suddenly back to being so proper, I feared a single glare might turn us all to stone."

She missed that very particular glance down his straight nose. The stern eyebrows. His mouth on her skin. The way he smiled at her, as if startled that he knew how.

She pushed the images away and tore a page out of the ledger, holding it to the candle's flame. The numbers burned, taking with them any threat of evidence. She would remember every addition, every subtraction, every guess. "He's gone back to his life, and me to mine."

"Did he hurt you?" Viola demanded.

Cat shook her head, smiling sadly. "I hurt him."

"Then apologize."

"I did. But I would do it again and he knows it."

"Hmph."

Cat took the last cask of brandy to the Jamaica Inn on Bodmin

Moor, hidden under cabbages. They ordered tea from her for her next delivery.

It was official. She was the smuggler of Little Crumpet.

And it would be enough. She would make it enough.

On the way back from the moors, she saw Penhallow, gray as a thundercloud on the cliff. Light flashed off the windows. Was Callum still inside? Was he sitting in his library, where he had pinned her to the settee and pleasured her until she screamed? Where she had betrayed him, the letters in her dress even as she writhed underneath him, eager for more? Had he spotted Bartholomew the turtle? The hawk on the roof? Had he visited the kittens?

Was he back in London even now, strolling through pleasure gardens, shopping on Bond Street? Would she see him one day, if she went to sell her lace? Would he even notice her?

Why couldn't she stop asking herself questions that had no answers? At least no answers that made her feel any better.

At least her luck in love was not contagious.

When she returned the cart to Ambrose and made her way back to the cottage, Viola was in the garden, showing Ruby her watercress garden and the rabbits that lived under the shed. Ruby stood out like an exotic hothouse flower in her silver silk dress, diamond drops at her ears. There was a one-eyed goat butting her knee and she laughed. Not so incongruous, after all.

She also held Viola's hand in hers, their heads tilted together as they whispered.

Cat knew that blush, that feeling of being outside of time.

They broke apart when Cat opened the gate. She refused to look at the garden wall, to remember Callum chasing her. It was hard enough not to see him at her kitchen table, eating Figgy 'Obbin.

"Cat!" Viola rubbed her hands on her skirt.

Ruby frowned as if Cat had run at them with a garden shovel.

She needn't have worried. Cat would never deprive her sister of happiness. She smiled. Viola's shoulders softened. She touched

Ruby's wrist. "I told you it would be fine."

Ruby blinked. "I am not used to a family such as yours."

Cat snorted. "No one else is likely to have a one-eyed goat."

"That's not what I meant."

"I know."

"Although, he is surprisingly darling."

Lady Ruby Chatsworth of Grosvenor Square, London, thought Seaweed, with his bad manners and frankly fragrant breath, was darling.

"Ruby has invited me to visit her in London," Viola said shyly.

Viola's dream had always been London.

"I see."

"Say you won't stop me."

"Of course, I won't."

"And I thought I might also bring some of your lace," Ruby added.

Cat stilled. She turned to her sister. Viola wrinkled her nose. "I had to tell her," she blurted out. "I needed her help keeping the custom agents distracted when Armstrong started asking for you."

"I told you not to do that. I had it in hand."

Viola rolled her eyes. "You are risking your life for us. The least I can do is flirt and dance a little."

"A little?" Ruby muttered.

Viola grinned. "Your secret is safe with her."

"I am the sole of discretion," Ruby agreed. "I do not gossip about true things."

"An interesting distinction."

Ruby shrugged. "London runs on gossip. Now, what do you say?"

It was exactly what Cat needed, but it still felt odd to discuss such things with a London lady wearing all her finery in their weedy garden.

"It's dangerous business," she warned her. "The punishment

for smuggling is hanging or transportation. Even for ladies, I imagine."

Ruby scoffed. "There is equal danger in a London ballroom, only the dagger goes through your back unbidden."

Cat shook her head. "This is not one of the duchess's games."

"Do you think I don't know that?" Ruby asked quietly. "And do you think I don't know how to hide or lie? My father, an earl full of his own esteem, is penniless. Entirely through his own doing, I might add. If you are terrible at gambling, you should find a new hobby."

Viola stepped closer, offering comfort.

"And what's the solution?" Ruby continued. "Marry me off to the highest bidder. I am not allowed to work, I have no useful skills beyond marrying well and making heirs. So let me do *this*. Because there is one more thing I can do, and that is to shop. Let me bring your lace to the most fashionable modistes in Town— because we both know Viola did not make it. They sell to women also trained to shop. Let us use their own blasted rules for our own good for once."

"My, that is a rousing speech."

"And without a dowry or marriage, we must find other means to make our way in the world," Ruby pressed on, incensed. "I will take care of your sister."

Viola nudged her. Hard. "We will take care of each other. And let your father and Mr. Armstrong keep their *dainty* women."

Cat grinned. "Hear, hear."

Perhaps it was madness to trust someone she knew so little about. But it was clear Viola was enamored and just as clear that Ruby had already been taking care of Viola, from horehound honey to dancing revenue men. And when the goat nibbled on the hem of her very elegant gown, she only smiled fondly. Seaweed was a very good judge of character. And fashion.

Cat withdrew one of the sealed letters from her pocket and handed it to Ruby. "Then I suppose you'll need this."

Ruby noticed the seal with some surprise. "Never say the duke is part of your operation."

"He is not."

"Ah."

"Thank you, Cat," Viola hugged her. "We won't let you down."

She returned the hug. "Just be happy. And write to me!"

Ruby paused before letting Viola show her the beach and her favorite spot to swim. "Oh, and Miss Sparrow?"

"Yes?"

"I won The Duchess Games."

"Congratulations."

"I think we tied," Viola argued. "Or would have, had I not fallen ill."

"Possibly. But the last dance of the night was mine." Her smile was smug, pointed. "The duke was miserable."

Chapter Thirty-Three

T HE DUKE OF Tremaine was covered in kittens.

It did not improve his disposition.

Much.

There was a certain comfort to the soft fur and the sharp inquisitive teeth. To the tiny meows as they clambered over him, searching for mischief. And treats. He caught one in his palm—Egg, he thought—before he tumbled off his knee and was rewarded with an instant rumble of purr. Egg was asleep before Callum had finished scooping him out of the air.

The kitchen was warm and smelled of bread and roast meats. A lamp burned on the grate, touching iron pans, jars of herbs, pots of salted butter. He had spent many hours here as a child when he was supposed to be sleeping. It always sorted him out. The warmth of it, the constancy. Cook's kindness under a layer of good-natured grumbling.

Kittens in the quiet kitchen should have been a reliable cure.

But they reminded him of Cat.

As did the entire kitchen. Setting raisins on fire for entertainment tended to stay with a person.

Everything reminded him of Caitriona Sparrow.

He needed to get out of this house. Out of Cornwall. Possibly England, altogether.

The sharp stab of pain had settled into an ache that would not be ignored. She had lied to him, had used his status for her own gain. Secretly. Flattering him like all of the others.

Truthfully, if he cared to think past the ache in his chest, she had never flattered him. She had practically pushed him into a pond. Had thrown kittens into his arms without permission. Had challenged him to a footrace, and then led him to a mess of rotted fish to challenge his ideas.

Had it all been a ruse?

The hours in his bed? In the library. He wouldn't believe that. His brain knew better. His heart wasn't so sure.

Frustration woke a growl in his throat. Egg batted him in reprimand.

Didn't she know he would have written a hundred letters with his ducal seal if she had just asked him?

He had lost her once when they were young. He didn't know if he could survive losing her again. Not now. Not like this.

Candlelight moved outside the door and there was a yelp. "Oh, you startled me, Your Grace!" Cook exclaimed. "What are you doing down here?"

He would never admit that his sister had sent him to the kitchen, much like a parent sending a troublesome child to bed early to sort out his manners.

"Couldn't sleep."

"Shall I warm you up some milky tea with honey?" She had made it for him often growing up, especially after another scolding lecture from his mother enumerating his faults as a future duke. At eight years old he had only wanted cake and maybe a paper boat to race in the fountain against his sister. Lessons on proper address, proper facial expressions, proper bows were hardly entertaining. Particularly as he appeared to do them all wrong.

"No, don't trouble yourself."

"Bah, won't take a minute." She bustled towards the kettle, filling it with water. "I was coming to fetch the wee beasties for their evening goat milk. Miss Sparrow was spot on with her suggestion to add gelatin. They've taken right to it. Don't mind telling you I wasn't sure Egg would get on but he's already proving himself a little warrior."

Egg, hearing her voice and the hiss of the kettle, lifted his head. One ear flopped. It was hard work being a kitten. Cook cooed and had all three kittens in her pockets and a mug of hot tea in Callum's hand before he could blink.

It was not as late as he'd hoped but the majority of the guests had gone home, and it was probably safe enough to hurry up the stairs. Dignified ducal walk be damned. He hadn't slept since the night of the ball, not for more than a few hours before he woke up disoriented, hard with want for Cat and miserable.

Definitely not *ducal* of him.

He'd never hated his title as much as he did right now.

His mother, of course, was furious. She had spent considerable time and money trying to force his hand, trying to find a duchess she approved. And he had wasted it. And that was before he'd even fallen in love with Cat.

In love with a girl from a fishing village with problematic ties to smuggling.

Armstrong was a lot of things, but he wasn't an idiot. If he'd suspected her, there was cause. More cause than he would ever know, having already dismissed most of the evidence due to her gender. He was tripping himself up and Callum had every intention of letting him. He might be furious with her, but no one put Cat in danger. No one. Not ever.

He would make sure it was very, very clear before he returned to London.

Glittering, crowded London with its never-ending parade of entertainment and diversions. With his cold empty house where all he could hear were carriage wheels on the cobbles and parties overflowing Grosvenor Square. He missed the sound of the sea when he was away. But he could not see himself staying here or returning often to be tortured. Nor could he imagine staying away.

Someone was in the billiards room; he heard the clack of the balls rolling across the green baize. Blackpool most likely. He wasn't in the mood for his friend's knowing smirks. Or his sister's. He picked up his pace.

"Caught," Summer sang out from the doorway.

Blackpool crossed behind her, cue in his hand. "Your sister cheats."

"I do not!"

"You bent over," he muttered. "In that dress."

Callum pinched his nose. "Blackpool, don't make me throw you out on your arse."

"That's not cheating," Summer argued, darting out to grab Callum's arm and dragging him inside.

A chandelier burned bright over the table and there were chairs along the wall for spectators. And whisky. Callum made a beeline for it, adding a dollop into his tea. And another. He felt Summer and Blackpool exchanging a glance behind his back. He turned, scowling. "What?"

Summer rolled her eyes at the set of his jaw. "Clearly, you need something stronger than kittens."

"Leave it, Summer."

"As if I would. Don't be absurd."

He sipped his tea, burnt his tongue, added more whisky.

"Honestly, Callum. You and Miss Sparrow are made for each other. Always have been. Anyone could see it. Why do you think our mother was so cross?"

"Besides the obvious?" Blackpool asked.

"Which is?"

"She's always cross."

"True."

Blackpool never said a harsh word about a woman. Not a lady, not a servant girl. Predictably, he took Cat's side. "I don't know what she did, mate. And I don't care. Neither does Summer. I've never seen you so wretched. Any moment, I expect you to start spouting bad poetry." He shuddered theatrically.

"Shut it."

"Get it sorted."

"She stole from me."

"If you tell me she stole your heart, I might gag."

"Jackass."

"There he is," Blackpool grinned. "I knew he was somewhere under all that ducal superiority." He nodded at Summer. "Your turn."

"Arsewit."

"I meant at billiards."

"Oh."

"Are you two quite finished?"

"I don't know, are you going to stay here and mope?" Summer shot back.

"I'm going to London."

"Like hell, little brother."

Callum scowled. "I wasn't asking permission."

She snorted. "Good, because you won't get it. You will not let our mother win. I forbid it."

"This isn't about Mother."

Summer rolled her eyes so hard she immediately rubbed her eyelids. "She's the one who convinced you that you had to be this paper doll version of a duke, all duty and discipline. Father knew how to laugh, at least."

"In all fairness, all of Mayfair probably had a hand in that," Blackpool put in.

"You're not helping," she snapped.

Callum rubbed his beard again, suddenly exhausted. "Neither are you," he informed his sister. "Though I know you mean to."

"I'm just saying you have more power than most people. Use it to grab your happiness with both hands. Idiot."

"She lied to me," he said quietly. "She used my title."

"Against you?"

He paused. "No." But she'd made his every doubt, every nightmare surface. That he wasn't good enough. That he was only a title. That he had to protect himself from everyone. If his mask cracked, the jackals descended.

That wasn't on her though. Summer was right. It was more complicated than that.

"Women have no options, little brother. You have the option of being morally righteous. She might not."

Cat had said something similar to him about rules and who they were made for.

"Did you ask her why she did it?" Summer pressed.

"Yes. No." He couldn't remember.

"Well, choose your pride or your heart, little brother."

"You make it sound simple." Why was there no whisky left in the damn decanter?

"Do you love her?"

Not a drop left. "Who?"

Summer narrowed her eyes. "I will bash you over the head with this stick."

"It's called a cue, love," Blackpool put in helpfully. They both ignored him.

"Do you love her?"

He wanted to say no. Wanted to say it didn't matter.

Instead, the truth came out in a snarl, nothing like the poetic lovers in storybooks.

"Of course, I love her."

Chapter Thirty-Four

IT WAS A beautiful day. Bright and calm and picturesque. The sea was a stunning blue, gulls wheeling above it. Wildflowers danced in the long grass, yellows and purples and pale pinks.

Cat would have punched it if she could.

She wanted rain and wind and dark threatening clouds eating the sky. She wanted everything the color of a bruise.

On top of everything else, Callum had made her melodramatic.

Damn the man.

She would not let regret and sorrow take away the pride and the sense of accomplishment that came from achieving the first part of her goal. A good portion of the contraband had been moved, some of it even already fenced. Viola had left for London at first light, and for the first time her pockets were not empty. Matthew had taken the dogs for a ramble in the fields and would then head down to the village, to negotiate with Angus for time in the forge. His wife had carried so many barrels that she had a considerable percentage of the incoming profit. Everyone was in a good mood.

Everyone but her.

And Juro.

She had walked the beach, visiting Rumpelstiltskin, a gull with a broken wing she had set last year. He stayed close to the cottage now, waiting for treats. She tossed pebbles in the waves until her arm ached. She did not cry.

Climbing back up the slipway, she heard a murmur of voices. But she was spoiling for a fight, so instead of hiding she marched over the crest of the cliff.

The sun shone behind four men, casting them in sinister silhouette. As she got closer, Juro smirked at her, flanked by Mr. Armstrong and two of his agents. She refused to show the chill of dread that snaked through her. Anything she had to hide was well and truly hidden. And she knew enough about Mr. Armstrong to know how to work around him. Daintily.

Juro, on the other hand was unpredictable and vindictive.

"Mr. Armstrong," she called out pleasantly, the wind whipping at her skirts. "How do you do?"

"Miss Sparrow, I'm afraid I come on Crown business."

Of course, he had.

She pasted a look of confusion on her face when she desperately wanted to growl like one of the dogs. "How can I help you?"

"We've had a tip that you might be hiding contraband."

She blinked, as though it was such a big word she could not quite understand it. The agents' postures softened. "Another tip? That is odd."

"Juro here was kind enough to direct us to your cottage."

"I'm sure he was."

"I'm afraid we must search the premises."

"Of course," she said, pushing open the front door. "Do come in."

After her dealing with Juro and his lads, she wasn't stupid enough to store the contraband in her cottage. Unfortunately, he wasn't stupid enough to assume she would either. And so he'd taken matters into his own hands.

The absolute tosspot.

The agents marched in behind her before she could do anything. The dogs were still out with Matthew. Juro had used that to his advantage before calling the revenue men. And she'd been stomping the beach in a fit of temper. She might have to punch herself as well.

"Sir," one of the agents said eagerly, pointing to the kitchen area.

Where the perfect summer day sunlight streamed through the window, landing right on the pale perfection of French lace.

As if she would keep ill-begotten French bloody lace piled in a basket by the fireplace. It was sloppy work and that offended her most of all. Juro would pay for that, above all.

Mr. Armstrong straightened his already military readiness. "Miss Sparrow, would you care to explain this French lace?"

"Yes," Juro drawled. "Do explain."

"Of course," she smiled again although her heart was racing, and her palms were starting to sweat. Dainty, she reminded herself. "My sister Viola is a skilled lacemaker. She will be most flattered that you thought her work fine enough to be French."

"Rubbish," Juro spat. "She can't have done all that."

There was quite a bit of it. She had no idea where he had found it, but she intended to keep every inch. It would fetch a pretty penny.

And luckily, she did not think Mr. Armstrong or his men knew the kind of time and work that went into making lace. It was enough that it was dainty, women's work. Which Viola had attempted for one winter before declaring she would cut all of her fingers off before doing again.

Thankfully, they had kept her bobbins.

"I can't think why someone would accuse us," she murmured, pulling out a worn wooden box filled with those bobbins. "But here are her tools."

All three agents peered into the box as though it contained a great mystery. Or possibly a snake. "May we speak to her?" Mr. Armstrong asked.

She was deeply grateful that her siblings were not here. It might be the only thing preventing her from outright murdering Juro. "I'm afraid she's gone to London to visit a friend," she said.

"Lady Ruby Chatsworth. I'm sure you remember her. She is a friend of the Duke of Tremaine."

"Ah," he said, eyes widening. "Very good, very good. We'll be on our way then."

Perhaps titles were good for something after all.

Juro did not agree.

"That's rubbish," he seethed. His plans had been thwarted and no one needed to tell her that he would keep at it. "Ask her what she's keeping in that cave down there."

Mr. Armstrong turned. "What cave?"

"There's a cave down there, nice and secret like."

"Miss Sparrow?"

"Of course, there is," she agreed. "This is Cornwall, after all. There are caves everywhere."

"Let's have a look then, and we can put this business behind us."

"Certainly."

When Juro smirked at her, she nearly smirked back. He had no idea.

They climbed down to the cave, Mr. Armstrong leading the way. He marched as though he was on a very important mission. "See," Juro crowed, shoving forward. "What's that then?"

"It's a barrel, sir," one of the agents whispered excitedly to Mr. Armstrong.

"A *smugglers* barrel," Juro insisted.

"I don't know what those look like," Cat said. "How do you?"

"We're going to have to open it," Mr. Armstrong said.

"I wouldn't suggest it," she answered.

Juro produced a crowbar, tucked in the back of his belt. He had come prepared. If only to smash her cottage to pieces, she was sure. "It's not safe here until you catch all the smugglers."

They crowded close, working at the tight lid. Something moved in the shadows behind them. Juro swore.

Sir Bartholomew ambled out of the cave, upholding his reputation for finding himself in odd places. He was no worse the wear from his altercation with Lady Siddal. Juro shifted, crowbar in his hand.

"Don't you dare," Cat said in the kind of voice general suited for haunted mansions where bodies turned up mysteriously murdered. He turned back to the barrel, muttering.

"Are you sure about this, Mr. Armstrong?" she called from the safety of the beach. She kept the turtle behind her.

"I insist."

It took a few moments of straining and grunting to pry the lid off. She knew, from the gagging and the howling, the exact second it popped off.

"God's teeth, what *is* that?"

"Cover it back up!"

One of the agents stumbled out, retching.

"Oh dear," she murmured.

"Miss Sparrow, why do you keep a bucket of fish heads?"

"It's fish slurry."

"It's utterly vile."

"That it is, which is why it's so far from the house. And the cave keeps it cool."

"What's it for?" Mr. Armstrong was well and truly horrified. He pressed a handkerchief to his nose. His eyes were watering.

"They use it to fertilize the fields," she explained. "It's hard to find honest work, so we do what we can."

Honestly, she had no idea if that was true. She'd heard it was a possible use, but she kept a bucket of rotting fish heads purely to discourage the revenue men. Callum's reaction to the stench of the pilchard palace had given her the idea.

One of the agents was still retching, a green cast to his face. The others were looking a little green too.

"I did warn you."

"I think we've seen enough," Mr. Armstrong said.

He and his men practically ran up the slipway.

Juro, regrettably, did not follow.

"Where's the goods?" he asked, anger marking his neck with

red splotches.

"I'm sure I don't know what you mean."

"I'm done playing games, you bitch."

She lifted her chin. "Go home, Juro."

She gave him a wide berth as she passed him to reach the path.

Not wide enough.

He grabbed her arm hard enough to bruise. She tried to jerk free. "Let go."

Instead, he threw her down onto the pebbles. Her elbow sparked with pain, her tailbone throbbed a warning. She tried to kick at his kneecap, but her feet tangled in her dress. And then he was upon her, spitting with rage.

His hands closed around her throat and squeezed.

She struggled for breath, clawing at his arms. His eyes bulged as he pressed harder over her windpipe. Searing pain worked up into her jaw, down into her chest.

He wasn't going to stop.

He meant to kill her.

Chapter Thirty-Five

THE FIRST TIME Juro screamed, it was because his ankle was in the vise of a snapping turtle's mouth.

The second time he screamed, it was because a duke was hurling him bodily through the air.

Cat sucked in air, her throat spasming. Tears blurred her vision and so she wasn't entirely sure what was happening until she heard Callum's voice, rough, gentle, furious but utterly controlled. "Cat, are you hurt?"

She tried to speak but squeaked instead. She swallowed gingerly, shaking her head.

"Breathe for me, siren." He brushed sand off her cheeks, tracked her tears, narrowed on the marks around her neck. Something snapped in his face. His eyes turned to dark ice, the kind that snaps your neck when you fall. He rose, every inch a duke. Every inch a predator.

When Juro screamed for the third time, it was short and strangled, choked in his own blood.

Callum punched like a brawler instead of an aristocrat, but he had the focus and the discipline of a duke. Juro got in a single punch, mostly through luck and the sheer size of him. Callum staggered back, spat blood, and then smiled.

The fight was short and vicious. Juro went down and could not gain ground again. Callum cracked his nose, then two teeth.

Juro's face turned red, purple and began to swell.

Callum kept punching him.

Cat crawled closer, her voice raspy but still functional. "Callum, stop."

After one more blow, Callum eased back, blood on his knuckles. His perfect cravat was rumpled. He stood, helping Cat gently to her feet. He angled himself so that not even Juro's rapidly swelling eyes could touch her.

"I won't bother warning you to stay away from her because I know damn well you will. You'll be transported by the end of the week, and should you think to come back, remember that they hang men who hurt duchesses."

Juro groaned and lost consciousness.

"Good riddance," Cat whispered.

"I'm taking you to the doctor," Callum added immediately. "Now. I'll carry you."

She smiled. "I don't need a doctor."

"You're seeing one. Two. Three at minimum," he insisted. "He was *strangling* you."

"Nothing a cup of tea can't cure."

He shook his head, stunned.

"Where did you even come from?" she asked.

"It doesn't matter, none of it matters. I was coming down here to argue with you some more, but seeing his hand around your throat—" He broke off, shuddering.

"I don't think he'll try that again."

His eyes glittered again. "He will not." He frowned. "What happened to his ankle?"

She grinned. She couldn't help it. "Sir Bartholomew bit him."

"He has more than earned his title as Sir. I think possibly he might be an earl."

"Lord Bartholomew. It does have a ring to it." She cleared her throat, feeling giddy, sore, slightly disoriented. And utterly, perfectly fine, and all because Callum was standing next to her. "I told you snapping turtles weren't to be underestimated."

"So you did. And so you are," he said. "Not to be underestimated."

She bit her lip. "I'm sorry, Callum. Truly."

"I love you. I've loved you for thirteen years," he said. "And I'm the one who should be sorry."

She stepped back, unsure. He was sorry for loving her? Could she blame him?

"I always told myself I would fight the world for you, would protect you from it, and when the time came, I could barely fight myself."

The ice she had been carrying inside her chest began to melt.

"I'm heartily ashamed, love."

"I'm the one who should be ashamed," she said.

"Not ever."

"I knew what I was doing."

"And you'd do it again."

She wrinkled her nose. "Yes, but differently."

He shook his head. "I love that about you." He kissed her cheek, the tip of her nose. "Please tell me I haven't ruined everything."

"If you tell me *I* haven't ruined everything."

"Be my duchess, Cat."

She blinked. "I couldn't," she said. "I'm a fisherman's daughter. A smuggler."

"And I'm a duke but you've never held it against me." He ran his hands up her arms. "You're already my duchess. You have been since that summer. You just never knew it."

She laughed, she couldn't help it. Happiness bubbled in her veins. "That seems like something I should have known."

"Unfortunately, my sister is right. I'm an idiot."

She laughed again. And then she kissed him because she didn't know what else to do with all of the emotions welling inside her. He kissed her back, stroking his big hand up her spine, digging his fingers in her hair. He nipped at her mouth, again and again until she forgot where they were.

On a smuggler's beach.

In Cornwall.

"Callum, I love you. I never stopped loving you. But I can't move to London." She tried to ease back.

He stopped her. "Good. I hate London."

"You can't mean it."

"I do mean it. Emphatically. And before you object any further and wound my ducal pride, just remember that I can keep Armstrong and his men in line."

She pretended to consider the matter. "That *is* true."

"What do you want? What do you need? Diamonds? Dresses? Horses?"

"God, no."

"Salt?"

She beamed at him. "Now that is the most romantic thing anyone has ever said to me." She kissed again, just because she could. "About that private beach of yours…"

"The cove where I first kissed you?"

"Yes. That's the one."

"What about it?"

"Don't you think it would make a splendid smuggling cove?"

"Done. Only the best for the Duchess of Smugglers. But if you're going to keep doing this, you are taking fencing lessons. Pugilism."

"Luckily, I hear you are an expert on lessons," she teased. "I suppose deportment and etiquette are on the list. For a duchess."

"Only if you want them."

"I suppose I need every weapon in my arsenal. And I've seen how you wield your title."

"I look forward to having my title serve me for once, instead of me blindly serving my title." He gripped her chin firmly, tilting her head to meet his gaze. "But we both serve *you*. Always."

"This can't really be happening," she murmured against his lips. "The Duke of Tremaine can't marry a smuggler."

"But Callum can."

"I did not win The Duchess Games," she said.

"True. Your painting really is dismal."

She grinned, poking him. "I beat you at the footrace."

He scoffed. Then he pressed his brow to hers. "Some games were worth playing.

Some games were worth winning. No matter the risk."

"Truly? Even if we do not wreck ships here, I am sure I will wreck your reputation."

"I don't care."

"You have cared about your reputation since before you could spell the word," she said dubiously. "You left Cornwall as soon as you got your title. You left me. Without a word."

"I'm sorry. God, Cat, if I could undo it."

"I didn't blame you. I still don't. Not really. I'm…just me."

"You are everything. Damn the title."

She stared. "You don't mean that."

"I do." His eyes flared hotter, willing her to believe him. "The title is a cold dead thing. You were the one who told me I should start wielding it better. And I intend to. It has received enough of my attention. I care what *you* think of me, Cat. Not the *ton*. Be mine, siren. Because I have always been yours."

"I was always yours too, Callum," she whispered. "But I never thought you'd be mine."

"Try and stop me."

"Your mother…"

He shook his head. "My mother will adapt or she won't. It's not like she will live with us."

"Are you sure? My family is just as… unique."

"I look forward to dog hair on all of the settees. I talked myself out of our happiness years ago and I won't let you do it now. Say yes. Say you'll be my duchess."

She smiled. "Yes."

The kiss deepened and seared through them, full of memories of bare salty skin and tangled limbs and soft moans. Of a summer in a secret cove, of nights in a dark library.

And interrupted by the sudden chorus of barking. Her dogs raced down towards her, neatly avoiding Lord Bartholomew who wandered away, dragging seaweed. Behind them, Matthew stopped at the bottom of the path, confused.

It wasn't every day you found your sister in the arms of a duke, a notorious bully unconscious at their feet, and a giant turtle meandering away.

About the Author

Alyxandra Harvey lives in an old stone house with her husband, multiple dogs, and a few resident ghosts who are allowed to stay as long as they keep company manners. She likes chai lattes, tattoos, and books. Sometimes fueled by literary rage.

Author of The Drake Chronicles, The Witches of London, Haunting Violet, Red, Love Me Love Me Not.

Twitter: AlyxandraH
Instagram: alyxandraharveyauthor